THE FORTUNES OF FINGEL

THE FORTUNES
OF FINGEL

SIMON RAVEN

Illustrated by
Michael ffolkes

BLOND & BRIGGS

First published in Great Britain 1976 by Blond & Briggs Ltd., London and Tiptree, Colchester, Essex. © *1976 Simon Raven. Printed by The Anchor Press Ltd., and bound by Wm. Brendon & Son Ltd., both of Tiptree, Essex.*

SBN 85634 055 3

Acknowledgement

Some of these stories were first published in the *New Statesman*, and the author acknowledges with thanks the permission of the Editor to print them here.

Contents

Fingle me, oh fingle me,
My patacake baby, come fingle me.

West Indian song

The Phantom Bawdy House

"Bloody marvellous it was," said Fingel to the group of subalterns round him, as we all waited for the Colonel to arrive. "If I hadn't seen it with my own eyes I should never have believed it. And I wouldn't expect you to believe it if I hadn't got Raven here as a witness."

I smirked and looked knowing.

"As soon as we came through the door," said Fingel, "we were offered champagne by a girl who was bare down to her midriff – and wearing only black stockings and garters below it. She led us through to a kind of seraglio . . ."

And so the tale went on. It had been Fingel's idea; it always was. Göttingen in 1952 was a charming place in which to be stationed, but, being a respectable university town, was definitely short on casual sex. So let us make their eyes goggle, Fingel had said to me one day, by inventing a sumptuous brothel. They'd want to believe in it so desperately that they'd lap it up. Fingel and I could then issue detailed instructions how to get there, and sit back to enjoy the subsequent annoyance.

"And another thing," Fingel was saying now, "some of those girls couldn't have been a day over eighteen . . ." In fact, he deposed, many of them must have been several years under it. What was more, Fingel inferred, they were blithely prepared to operate in groups, to organise unusual spectacles, and to cater for curious whimsy. He's overdoing it, I thought. Some of his audience were beginning to look sceptical; they had been had by Fingel before. But Fingel was master of the situation. And then the bugles sounded for dinner. Fingel's work was done. I could see it in their eyes. "They're going to bite," said Fingel in my ear, as we walked along the corridor, down a line of drummers drumming, to the dining-room.

And bite they did. After dinner they came in twos and threes, rather drunk now, wanting to know how to get there. Fingel gave them the instructions which he and I had worked out on the ground the previous evening, instructions which would eventually bring his victims to a particularly loathsome public urinal somewhere miles beyond the railway station. Carefully the subalterns listened, doomed men; and then, furtively euphoric, set out into the night.

The next morning at breakfast, Fingel and I were rewarded by the sight of row on row of frustrated and scowling faces. Fingel had done it again.

"I hope you all enjoyed yourselves," he said.

"Yes," said an unexpected voice, "I did; and thank you for the tip."

The speaker was the newest joined National Service second lieutenant, who was called Dave Jones, refused to answer to the more passable "David", and was not considered to be "the sort of chap we want in the mess".

"Lovely it was," said Jones. He gave a long and circumstantial account of what he had done in Fingel's bordello ("Can't think how the rest of you missed it, I found it easily enough") and concluded with the boastful claim that the girl had let him off at half-price, as she herself had enjoyed it quite as much as Jones had.

"We can't let him get away with *that*," said Fingel later in the morning, as we sat by the fire in his Platoon Office. "Horrid little National Service man with spots and specs and

Brylcream, finessing me and showing off like that. We must teach him a lesson."

The next morning at breakfast there were more cross faces. Encouraged by Jones's story, several subalterns had set out yet once more to find Fingel's paradise, with, of course, the same lugubrious and squalid journey's end at the public urinal.

"Raven and I went last night," announced the beaming Fingel. "Didn't we, Simon?" I nodded.

"Can't think how all you other fellows keep failing to spot the place."

"I didn't fail, the time I went," Jones said smugly.

"Which reminds me," said Fingel. "The Madame sent a message up for you, Dave. 'Tell that little chap who was here last night,' she said, 'that Herr Doktor came round inspecting this morning and found that the girl he went with' – *your* girl, Dave – 'has got clap.' The Madame's very sorry, and hopes you'll be lucky."

Dead silence. Now, it had been Fingel's intention to subject the wretched Jones to several minutes' horrified and humiliating scrutiny from his brother officers, and then finally and publicly to demolish his whole fantasy, thus revealing that Jones, while he couldn't possibly have clap because there was nowhere he could have caught it, was nevertheless and by the same token a nasty, bragging little fibber. We had expected Jones to exhibit anger or embarrassment when the fictitious Madame's fictitious message was delivered: what we had not expected was that he should turn ashen with shock and start sweating with terror.

"Come outside," he gibbered at me and Fingel. And once outside: "Jesus Christ. Clap you said. Whatever can I do?"

"Don't be silly," Fingel said. "You know as well as I do that neither the place nor the girl exists."

"But they *do* exist," wailed Dave Jones.

And then he told us how, more patient than the others, he had lingered in a street near the urinal; how at last a door had opened, a hand had come out and beckoned . . . "It wasn't as grand as you'd described it," said Jones, "but then I always thought you were playing that side up a bit, and it wasn't too bad at that. My girl certainly wasn't as young as eighteen, but she wasn't that old either, and she was pretty good at it. And of course that was a lie about her letting me off cheap, but I did go there, Fingel, and I did do what I did and now you say the Madame says that I've probably caught clap."

"I tell you," said Fingel, "that my place doesn't exist and neither does my Madame. Your place must be another place – a *real* place which by some coincidence is near my imaginary one. So of course you haven't got clap, Davy boy. That's all made up. But," added Fingel, "it seems my creative instinct was right. There *is* a cathouse in that area, and you've been there, and now you're going to tell us all about it."

So Dave Jones told us all about it. It wasn't all that grand, as he'd already said, but it was clean and neat inside, and the girls had been quite jolly – round about thirty, most of them must have been – and it had been indicated that he could have two to himself but one had been enough, because although the price was very reasonable a National Service second lieutenant's pay did not go very far. And so on. No champagne, Jones said, only beer; but comfortable rooms with lots of mirrors which the girl was clever at using – all in all excellent value, he thought, now that he no longer had reason to suppose he'd caught the clap. A thoroughly admirable, if modest, establishment . . . and here was the address. Just past the celebrated urinal, a turning on the right, about thirty yards down: No 17.

"We'll go and take a look tonight," said Fingel later in the morning, warming his bottom at his office fire. "What a piece of luck. That Jones creature is good for something after all."

So immediately after dinner we set off. A taxi to the station, a tedious walk through labyrinthine back streets, the urinal at last, a turning just past it on the right, thirty yards down . . . and No 17. Fingel knocked. The door opened. A pretty woman in her late twenties appeared, looked us up and down, and, smiled pleasantly.

"As the poker descended on Fingel's head, I fled."

"Meine Herren?" she said.

"We've come to spend the evening," said Fingel, whose German was as feeble as my own.

"Mein Herr?"

"You know," said Fingel. "Jig-a-jig. Er . . . um . . . Zig-zig. That is . . . *pour faire l'amour.*"

The girl nodded politely. "*Moment,*" she said.

She walked back through the hall, and spoke rapidly in German through an open door.

"Ah," said Fingel as an old woman waddled into the hall, "this will be the senior bawd. What is the German for 'I would like three of your girls all at once'?"

"*Drei mädchen mit mir zusammen?*" I suggested tentatively.

The old woman stopped in front of us. "Jig-a-jig?" she said. "Zig-zig?"

"Ja," said Fingel, trying his best. "*Drei mädchen mit mir zusammen, bitte.*"

As the poker descended on Fingel's head, I fled through the front door.

"Luckily," said Fingel, when I went to see him in the sick bay, "I've managed to persuade the Colonel it was all a misunderstanding. I was only asking to use her telephone, I told him, to call a taxi. Taxi: zig-zig. They sound a bit the same if you twist you mouth about. I hear he's got the police to believe it. They still think of us as an occupying power, do you see. Very servile, these Krauts, once they've been beaten."

"That old woman wasn't servile."

"No. I wonder how Dave Jones could have made that mistake. He seemed so clear, so accurate. No 17, he said."

"He swore to me later on that he said No 7."

"Oh. Been there yet?"

"Yes."

"How was it?"

"I'm lucky," I said, "not to be lying there next to you. At No 7 it was a flat-iron instead of a poker."

"You mean . . . Jones has been having us on?"

"Evidently."

"I could have sworn he was terrified about the clap. I was sure he'd had a girl somewhere, so of course I believed in his brothel."

"So did I. We've been out-fingelled, Fingel."

Hot Chocolate

"Annoying scene at the Alte Krone last night," Fingel said. "The Head Waiter told me I couldn't have any more credit."

"So how did you pay him?"

"I didn't. He was prudent enough to make his announcement before I started eating. I had to go on to the Schwarz Hof. Pretty poor grub, but I think I can screw three or four more dinners out of them before they start asking for cash."

"What then?" I enquired.

"You have a point, old bean. I'm rapidly running out of restaurants. But as I was leaving the Alte Krone, the proprietor popped up and told me a very interesting thing. He appreciated my custom, he said, or would do if it could only be put on a more stable basis, and he would like me to consider a suggestion: cocoa."

"What?"

"Cocoa. Although the war's been over for seven years, that's a thing they're still very short of. All the old BAOR markets – whisky, cigarettes, sugar – are as dead as last Friday's fish, but they are still short of cocoa, and they badly want it to make those glutinous great cakes which Krauts are so fond of. In short, if I find a nice big consignment of cocoa, the proprietor of the Alte Krone will look on my signature with respect for many moons to come."

"And just where would you find this consignment?"

"Company stores. All companies carry a large supply of cocoa for use on training and manoeuvres – the Army Council does not approve of rum issues, these days, and cocoa's the coming thing instead. So tons of cocoa are sitting in the company stores – and my old chum, Sergeant Sweenie Mack, is sitting on top of the cocoa. They've just made him Acting Colour Sergeant while the proper man's off on a course. I think I shall find Sweenie quite cooperative."

"Look," I said; "the bottom may have dropped out of the old black markets in whisky and so on, but the SIB is still keeping an eye cocked and they know as well as you do that the Krauts are keen on Army cocoa. The penalty for trading in it is to be cashiered and probably imprisoned."

"Better cashiered than starved," Fingel said.

*　　*　　*　　*　　*　　*

"Be my guest," said Fingel a week later, as we sat down at a corner table in the Alte Krone, under a huge gilt crown draped about with crimson velvet. "Nothing on this menu is beyond the means of Fingel."

"Right, I'll start with Fresh Beluga Caviar."

"So shall I. Odd that they should be able to get fresh caviar and yet have such trouble over common cocoa. It would have done your heart good to see how grateful the proprietor was when I delivered."

"How much did you deliver?" I asked.

"Mack reckoned we could get away with five of those enormous cans of the stuff."

"You mean you carted five bloody great cans out of barracks? In full sight of the Regimental Police?"

"Of course not. We emptied the cans into three kit-bags, and I then took my platoon on a special training run with full kit-bags slung over shoulders. Straight past the guard and through the gate. The Colonel looked out of his window and was mightily impressed with our performance."

"So now you've involved your platoon?"

"Only three select men who carried the kit-bags with the cocoa, and *they* were so grateful to sit around in the Alte Krone guzzling beer and sausage while the rest of the platoon were still running that I shan't have any bother from them. A more serious problem is Sweenie Mack. He wanted twenty-five per cent of the profit and was not at all pleased when I told him I was not being paid in cash."

Sergeant Mack came in with a crony and sat down at the far end of the room.

"So I arranged free feeding facilities for him too," Fingel said. "A great nuisance, having Other Ranks in one's favourite restaurant, but there was no other way."

"More to the point," I said: "how are you and Mack going to replace that cocoa before someone comes round the stores to check on it?"

"Not too difficult, old bean. Every time I take my platoon out on a route march or something I'll sign for an issue of cocoa but won't draw it. Even when I'm *not* going out on training I can sign for the odd issue. We'll account for it that way."

"It might look rather odd – column after column of your signature in the book."

"I'll get other chaps to sign for fake issues. Pay 'em all back with dinner here."

"At that rate you won't be welcome here very long. There's a limit to what you can expect for three kit-bags of cocoa."

"Don't be such a blister. It's my Beluga you're eating. Anyway," said Fingel, squeezing a little lemon juice lovingly on to the luscious grey eggs, "I may be in funds again soon. I'm next in line to be made up as Temporary Captain – "

" – *If* there's a vacancy – "

" – And then I could afford to buy cocoa in bulk from England and replace what we've taken from the stores."

"*When* the Pay Corps got round to paying you the increase. Which would take them about four months."

"At least there'd be pretty solid arrears when they did come across. And if time starts pressing, I could order a lot of cocoa on tick from Fortnum and Mason."

"You only got out of England twelve hours ahead of Fortnum and Mason's last writ."

"I'll start an account in another name. Yours, perhaps."

"Look, Fingel," I said: "the real danger, as you very well know, is that someone may come round to do a spot-check on that cocoa in the stores at any minute of any day. So let's stop having fantasies about Captain's pay or swindling Fortnum and Mason, and ask ourselves what happens if some nosey-parker turns up to take a gander at 0830 hours tomorrow."

"Acting Colour Sergeant Mack will fob him off. Sweenie will be able to produce the correct number of cocoa cans, as we kept those we'd emptied and have since filled them up with light dry earth topped off by layers of genuine cocoa."

"Dear God. That old trick."

"It's a good trick or it wouldn't be an old one."

"But any nosey-parker who knows his job digs down to take samples from the bottom."

"Not if Sweenie Mack is showing him his new set of naughty pictures from Berlin."

"Fingel. It could very well be the Colonel himself coming round to inspect. Don't tell me Mack is going to beguile *him* with naughty pictures from Berlin."

"I admit," said Fingel, "that there may be extreme cases in which it will be necessary to improvise."

"Trust to luck, you mean."

"Fortune favours the bold. Do admit, old bean, that contraband training run was an operation of genius."

Sergeant Mack clumped across from his table and came officiously to attention by ours.

"A vurra good evening to Your Honour," he now deposed to Fingel.

It was Mack's custom to apostrophise Fingel (and only Fingel) quite frequently in this absurdly antiquated style.

20

Whether he did it out of reverence, irony or sycophancy was a nice matter for speculating. Myself I inclined to the view that "Your Honour" on Mack's lips conveyed warning mixed with covert mockery; for although the phrase was always uttered with apparent respect, it always came out at times when Fingel was either threatened with humiliation and disgrace or had recently and narrowly evaded them.

"And a good evening to you, Sergeant Mack," Fingel now said. "As you see, I am eating my dinner."

"And I wouldna wish to spoil Your Honour's evening," said Mack, "not for the whole wide wurld. But I thought I should apprise Your Honour I have wurd along the bush-wire that the Captain Quartermaster his ane sel' is checking on all company stores tomorrow."

Fingel's face juddered. The Quartermaster Captain was a very old soldier of acid insights, scholarly exactitude and unbreachable integrity.

"What time?" Fingel said.

"The Good Lurd alone kens, Your Honour, and foreby not even He. This is a snap inspection, and it's lucky we are to be warned of it at all. Am I to have Your Honour's instructions the noo?"

Fingel gazed down at the rich grey Beluga on his plate.

"Foreby the owner of this restaurant could lend us the cocoa back for a wee while?" suggested Mack. "He cannot yet have used it all for his cakies."

"He'll have used quite a lot," said Fingel, "and almost certainly have sold some at a high price elsewhere. Besides, we shall look such bloody fools if we ask for it back now."

"Better fools than felons," said Sergeant Mack.

"I do believe you're losing your nerve, Sweenie."

"I dinna wish to lose my stripes – any more than Your Honour wishes to part with those two pretty stars on each shoulder."

"Look," said Fingel. "One way or another, most of that cocoa will have gone and cannot be got back now. Our only plan must be to convince the QM that those five cans of earth

21

in your stores contain genuine cocoa. The only way he will find out that they do not contain genuine cocoa will be by digging down under the layers on top. Right?"

"And how am I to stop him? I dinna think the QM will be lured from his duty by those sinful pictures from Berlin."

"Too true he won't be." Fingel looked down again at his caviar. "I saw a film a year or two ago," he said, "called *Kind Hearts and Coronets*. Someone sends a general a pot of Beluga caviar, and when the general digs into it, it blows his head off. Just beneath a thin covering of Beluga, you see, there was a bomb which the general's spoon had detonated. Now then: when the QM pushes his scoop through the top layer of genuine cocoa in the first of those cans – "

" – Heaven forfend ye'll have put a bomb there," said Sergeant Mack, glowing with excitement at the notion.

"No," said Fingel, "that would be overdoing it. But I have a scheme rather along those lines. Meet me in the company stores, Sergeant Mack, at eleven o'clock tonight. Have those cans out, open and ready for me, and I will make it all very plain to you."

*　　*　　*　　*　　*　　*

"It worked a real dream," Fingel told me early next morning at breakfast.

"What did?"

"My plan to fool the QM about that cocoa."

"But the check-up hasn't even happened yet."

"I know, old bean."

"Then how can you have fooled the QM?"

"It's like this," Fingel said. "Although I made a show of confidence to you last night about my ability to replace all that cocoa, I must confess that I have been finding the problem rather a worry. So a day or two ago I devised a plan which might, with a bit of luck, settle the matter here and now. The first stage was to start a story about an impending inspection of stores and make sure it got to Sweenie Mack and put the wind up him."

"So today's check-up is nothing more than a rumour?"

"Precisely. There'll be one sooner or later, of course – "

" – Probably sooner – "

" – Probably sooner, I agree, but not, to my knowledge, today. *That's* just a barrack-room buzz, got up by me, to make Mack start pissing his knickers."

"From what I saw of him in the Alte Krone, you'd clearly managed that."

"As soon as he came over to our table, I knew I was in business. The next stage was to convince him straightaway that I'd thought of a wheeze to cope with the QM. Hence that spiel about the caviar bomb in *Kind Hearts and Coronets*. Sweenie's a shrewd man, but he's also very romantic in rather an infantile way, and he has great belief in bizarre escapes and contrivances – the sort of thing he's forever reading about in boys' magazines like *Hotspur*. So when I told him I was going to bug those cocoa cans one way or another, I knew his curiosity would get the better of him and I'd have him exactly where I wanted him. And sure enough, there he was in the company store at eleven o'clock last night, waiting for me, with the cans all opened up and ready for me to go to work on. God alone knows what he thought I could possibly be going to do with them, but he'd taken my bait and there he was – when in comes a party of Regimental Police, tipped off anonymously by Fingel, and catches Mack red-handed – or so it appears – fiddling the company cocoa under cover of darkness. So what happens next?"

"Mack flashes those dirty pictures at them."

"That's right, old bean. And since the party is headed by a young corporal of little experience, they all sit down and drool over the pictures, while Mack passes round an enamel mug full of neat whisky and starts to sweet-talk them all into believing that he's been working late in the stores and is checking the cocoa, not fiddling it. Just about then – enter Fingel. 'What is this disgraceful scene?' cries Fingel: 'the piquet half-drunk on duty and goggling at disgusting pictures. Sergeant Mack, you should know better than to use your store as a pot-house. And anyway what are these cocoa cans doing, opened up like that' – prod, prod – 'why, they're full of earth, just what is the meaning of *this*? 'Fore God, I have discovered a conspiracy to defraud Her Majesty.'

"At this the young corporal breaks down and sobs, 'Sir, kind sir, I know nothing about it.' Fingel then expatiates sternly on the enquiry that must now ensue if he does his duty and impounds the cans as evidence. Every sort of charge will be urged against every man in the room (including himself, though only he and Mack know *that*), and drunkenness on piquet *alone* will be enough to break the corporal and put his comrades behind bars for a month, *et cetera, et cetera, et cetera*. But then, amid the mutters of fear and shame, Fingel suddenly smiles a warm, human, radiant smile. There might yet be a way out, Fingel concedes. If the cocoa cans were to be totally and immediately disposed of, and if a plausible explanation were forthcoming to account for their disappearance, there could never *be* an enquiry about what was inside them or who put it there, and the various misdemeanours of all present would remain for ever hidden. After all, says Fingel, what are a few cans of cocoa, that they should ruin the promising careers of six young soldiers and bring disgrace on that much loved figure, Sergeant Mack? Follows a cleverly deployed tear or two from Mack and protests of boozy gratitude from the police piquet – who are, however, quite sober enough to implement Fingel's plan. They fetch the Regimental Police wagon, cart away the cocoa cans and many other valuable items of equipment, slam them deep into the incinerator, and then wake the Orderly Officer. Their story is absolutely pat and supported by all six of them. They were on a routine patrol, saw a suspicious light in D Coy stores, went to investigate, and found the door open but not so much as a cat moving. Leaving a guard on the door, they had roused Acting Colour Sergeant Mack from his innocent slumbers in the Sergeants' Mess; Mack had deposed that such and such items, including five cans of cocoa, were gone; and now, would the Orderly Officer kindly come to the scene and take official cognisance of what had occurred?

24

"Later this morning," continued Fingel, helping himself to about half a pound of marmalade, "the barracks will be searched for the missing stores and their remains will eventually be found in the incinerator – where, it will be assumed, the thieves put them in panic. Seven compasses, six pairs of binoculars, four revolvers, fourteen blankets – and five barely recognisable cans of what had once been cocoa, all stolen and incinerated by persons unknown – and who never will be known. Thus the cans will be duly accounted for and officially written off, and we need think no more of making up stock from Fortnum and Mason. The episode is entirely closed – apart from the banquets which I shall continue to enjoy at the Alte Krone."

I thought for some minutes.

"Surely," I said at last, "you and Mack could have managed the thing between you. No need to rig up all that tricksy intrigue with the Regimental Police."

"We needed independent witnesses," said Fingel, "and we needed strong men to hump all that gear about without arousing suspicion. The Regimental Police – even a corporal's piquet – go where they like unquestioned. But imagine me and Mack rushing to the incinerator with a vehicle full of stores in the middle of the night – a sight as obvious and as guilty as a nine-month belly at the altar."

"Well, you might at least have taken Mack into your confidence from the beginning. He must have had a very nasty shock when the piquet caught him mucking about with those cans."

"Indeed he had, and he has complained to me most bitterly about it. But that," said Fingel, "was the most refined element in my whole scheme. By springing a crisis on Mack, I brought out the best in him – by putting his back up against the shit-house wall, where rats like him are always at their most resourceful. And at the same time, old bean, I have ensured that he will no longer annoy me by haunting the Alte Krone. Having been brought so close to scandal by my machinations, he now knows that although he is officially in the clear he cannot risk incurring notice by living at unnatural expense."

"The same might be said of yourself."

"For me, old bean, the Alte Krone is a *natural* expense. People expect me to go there even when I can't afford it and will only start noticing me if I *don't*. But for Mack it is a *conspicuous* expense; the Alte Krone is not for the likes of him if he wants to avoid remark. In short, old bean, the present exigencies of discretion require me to enjoy myself and Mack to deny himself. An amusing and convenient instance of what is known as social injustice."

Fingel's Artillery

"A message for Your Honour," said Sergeant Mack: "from the Adjutant's Office."

Fingel slit open a buff envelope and extracted a flimsy sheet of paper.

"Great piles of crap," Fingel said: "my new guns are here. Waiting at the station. 'Lieutenant Fingel, as O/c Anti-Tank Platoon'," he read from the order in his hand, " 'will proceed immediately to Göttingen Station to take on charge from the Bahnhof Direktor five 120 millimetre Anti-Tank Rocket Launchers and will cause them to be conveyed to these Barracks forthwith'."

"Well, what about it?" I jeered. "Those guns were bound to arrive sooner or later. You ought to be full of joy and enthusiasm. Now you'll have a proper Anti-Tank Platoon at last instead of those absurd wooden toys."

"We couldna hope," said Sergeant Mack, "to get away with just the one gun for ever."

This conversation was going on in Fingel's Anti-Tank Platoon Office at Border Barracks, Göttingen, in the early autumn of 1953. The previous spring, much to Fingel's delight, his six cumbrous old Seventeen Pounder guns had been withdrawn, while because of some hiatus of a kind common in military affairs only one of the new type of Anti-Tank weapon had been issued in lieu. The remaining five, pending their arrival, were represented for tactical purposes by five token objects made of plywood and correspondingly easy to manipulate. Thus, during the whole of the summer season of training and manoeuvres, Fingel and the forty-odd men of his platoon had only one piece of genuine ordnance to deploy and maintain, even by Fingel's standards an unexacting task. But now –

" ' – Lieutenant Fingel is reminded'," Fingel read from the order, " 'that the Annual Administration Inspection by the GOC this Division is only seventy-two hours away, and that the five new Rocket Launchers on his charge must be cleaned, assembled, and rendered fully operational before the Inspection commences'."

"They'll be wrapped in rotten sacking," said Sergeant Sweenie Mack, who adored this style of disaster, "with the barrels stuffed along solid with the grease and the detachable fittings clankering about on the loose and an inch deep in rust. There'll be wee bitty nuts and bolts gone missing all over, and the tyres will be as flat as a Hebrew's loaf. The sights will be smashed and the firing levers will be warped and the towing brackets will – "

" – For Christ's sake shut up," said Fingel, " and try to be helpful."

" 'Fully operational', that order says," continued Mack in a meditative tone, "which among all else, as Your Honour well kens, means that the crews must be fully trained to shoot them off. Foreby a summer spent faffing aboot with plywood will not have been the best preparation for that, I'm thinking; and when the General Officer Commanding this Division asks to see a little Gun Drill (for he's an old Artillery hand, they do say, and dearly loves a sight of cannon) there'll be such a looning and a clooning that Your Honour will be arrested on the spot."

"And so will my Platoon Sergeant," Fingel snarled at

Sweenie Mack; "I promise you that. So if you don't want to find yourself back in the Men's Canteen, Sergeant Mack, drinking thin brown beer with never a chaser of whisky in sight and flushed out by the Orderly Corporal at 9 p.m. sharp every evening of your miserable life, you'll scour up those Scottish wits of yours and think what we'd better do next, before both of us are swimming in shit."

*　　*　　*　　*　　*　　*

"Glad those guns of yours have got here at last," said the Colonel to Fingel at luncheon in the mess; "looks much better than having those silly wooden jobs."

"I'm afraid there's been a hitch, Colonel," said Fingel glumly.

"What hitch? Your orders were quite plain: you were to go and see that German Bahnhof chappie on the *jilde* and bring those guns back to barracks. Then get 'em cleaned up, and all *thik hai.*"

"Things weren't quite *thik hai* at the station, Colonel. I went off to see that German Bahnhof chappie within fifteen minutes of receiving the order. The guns weren't there."

"*Weren't there?*"

"Weren't there, Colonel. Jolly bad show."

Fingel lifted a silver goblet (presented by Captain Percival Boffingham-Bramble in Seringapatam in 1889), held it briefly in front of the Colonel's face as if toasting him, and took a long swallow.

"I've got a letter of apology from the Bahnhof chappie," Fingel went on as he lowered the goblet. "He's in a terrible flap, looking high and low. He swears they'd come in yesterday evening, when he notified the Adjutant's Office about them, and of course he'll let us know at once if he finds them again."

"All I can say is, he'd better find them in time for the Inspection."

"Perhaps he will, Colonel; and then again, perhaps he

won't. We must hope for the best. Here's his letter of apology, by the way – just for the record."

* * * * * *

"All right," I said to Fingel later that afternoon, having dropped in to warm my bottom at the stove in his office, "what really happened?"

"What I told the Colonel, old bean. That Bahnhof chappie couldn't find me so much as a single gun in his station; so eventually he had to give up and write a grovelling chitty of confession."

"But it's incredible. He can't just have lost five Anti-Tank guns."

"You wouldn't think so, old bean. But I rather think there's been an unfortunate misunderstanding over the goods wagons. You see, while I went to the Bahnhof chappie's office to open up negotiations, Sergeant Mack did a little recce round the place, and there in a siding was a wagon labelled British War Department Stores (BAOR) NACH GOETTINGEN. Our baby, thinks Sergeant Mack; so now we know where it is that label had better come off. Bad for security, he thinks, because some casual spy might fancy a peep at those British War Department Stores, and we can't have folk like that spotting our new Rocket Launchers. And just to make security doubly secure, he thinks, I'll pop on another label I happen to have with me which says STUHLEN NACH FRANKFURT. No spy will want to look at a wagonful of chairs, he thinks, and even if he does, and finds our guns instead, he'll think they're going to Frankfurt and that will confuse him. So then Sergeant Mack suddenly has to go for a strain in the Herren, and as he hurries back he sees a wagon labelled STUHLEN NACH FRANKFURT being attached to a long line of other wagons also labelled FRANKFURT. Oh dear goodness me, he thinks, I hope that's not our wagon; but lo and behold, when he gets back to the siding, our wagon has gone."

Fingel paused and gave a long, sorrowful sigh.

"Poor silly Sergeant Mack! He has not been very adroit, I'm afraid, but since he so evidently took his precautions out of good will and a sense of duty, I cannot find it in me to make a fool of him by reporting him to the Colonel or explaining what has happened to the Bahnhof chappie. Meanwhile, however, I greatly fear that this wretched misunderstanding will considerably hamper the search for our guns, and I must sadly predict," concluded Fingel, "that they will not be delivered to us in time for the Annual Inspection – if indeed" – he rolled his eyes to heaven – "they have not been lost for ever."

Fingel in the Field

"You hang around here tonight," said Fingel, "and you'll see some fun when the retreat begins. I'm going to need you." There was a loud, crackling bleat; Fingel turned with a pout of distaste and picked up a pair of earphones. "Fingel here," he said, disdaining every known law of correct wireless procedure, "what's the matter now?"

Fingel and I were sitting in a kind of caravan, which had been dug into a hole in the middle of a copse and was heavily draped with camouflage nets. The interior of the caravan was plastered with maps of West Germany and comprehended a battery of radio transmitters, over one or the other of which Temporary Captain and Adjutant Fingel would from time to time relay a languid instruction or improvise an evasive answer.

We were in the middle of Exercise Broomstick, which was the climax of our mid-summer manoeuvres for 1954 and was to take the form of a retreat by night from our present position to the Lüneburg Heath to a destination as yet unknown. The Colonel had just been summoned to Brigade HQ to receive final orders, the Second-in-Command, an old India hand, was having his siesta, and thus our entire battalion was for the time being under the somewhat dilettante control of Fingel.

". . . How should I know where your rations have got to?" Fingel was saying on the set. "Perhaps they've been captured by the enemy." A harassed voice started to reply, but Fingel pulled a plug out from somewhere and the set went dead. "I think we'll have radio silence for a while," Fingel said; "all this silly chatter over the air is bad for security. What was I saying?"

"That you'll need my help tonight when the retreat starts. But what about my guns?" Being the new commander of the Anti-Tank Platoon, I was personally responsible, as Fingel well knew, for gathering up my six anti-tank guns from their outlying positions and getting them into their correct place in the retreating column.

"Bring them in now," said Fingel: "I'm going to need them too."

"But they're not meant to be brought in till after dark. That's the whole point of this exercise."

But Fingel had already put the plug back into the transmitter. "Attention all sub-units," he said. "Instruct anti-tank guns in support to withdraw and RV at Battalion HQ immediately." He pulled the plug out again. "When they get here," he said to me, "hide them in that hollow beyond this copse."

"But I don't understand."

"Only have faith," said Fingel, "and all will be made plain."

The afternoon went on. One by one my guns arrived and were duly concealed, with the heavy-tracked vehicles that drew them, in the hollow adjacent to the copse. The Second-in-Command stirred in his deck chair as they rumbled past but did not wake. Later on the Colonel arrived back from Brigade HQ. Fingel hurriedly replugged the radio transmitter. The Second-in-Command was woken at last and sent off, sweaty and disagreeable, to reconnoitre the area to which Brigade had now ordered us to retreat. Company commanders were summoned to an O-group, and all complained that they

34

had been unable to contact HQ on the wireless for the entire afternoon.

"The set went kaput," said Fingel. "I've just finished mending it."

Orders were given. Darkness would fall at 2142 hours, at which time precisely companies would commence withdrawal. A Coy to pass through the check point at 2157 hours, B Coy . . . etc., etc., etc. The company commanders dispersed. Evening came on. The Colonel had a quick and nasty sandwich, and went off to supervise the manning and organisation of the check point (a crossroads about a mile away).

"Remember," he said to Fingel, "you and the command trailer and the other HQ vehicles are due through the check point at 2225 hours. You'll have your hands full getting them all dug out in time, so get started at once."

"Yes, Colonel," said Fingel.

"Now," he said to me over a bottle of hock and a large dish of stuffed quails, which were elegantly served to us by his batman a few minutes after the Colonel's departure, "it is 2105 hours. At 2145 we shall have visitors."

"Visitors?"

"That beastly Brigadier and his syncophants will come snooping round to see how we are getting on with our preparations to withdraw. His great object will be to make sure that all officers assist in digging out the vehicles."

This sounded likely enough. The Brigadier, a lean, mean, ambitious officer, was well-known for his modishly "democratic" approach to soldiering. Officers, he insisted must do their full share of menial labour in the field and must dress exactly as their men did, in ammunition boots, steel helmets, webbing equipment and all.

"Lewson from Brigade warned me," Fingel went on. " '2145 hours he's got your HQ scheduled for,' Lewson said, 'and he'll come in battle order and tin hat himself so as to mingle unnoticed with the crowd and get a closer look. So make sure you're in there digging with the troops'."

"And shall you be?"

"No. I have an amusing plan for a Brigadier bate. He particularly loathes me and will be particularly keen to catch me skiving. On that the plan turns."

"And where do I and my guns come in?"

Fingel told me. I then went over to the hollow to pass on his instructions to my sergeant and returned to the caravan, where Fingel, now in an advanced state of excitement, had changed from battle dress into a sleek service dress tunic and highly polished Sam Browne belt. He was carrying a riding whip.

"Rather overdoing it?" I said. "That whip?"

"As Adjutant, I am a mounted officer."

"Temporary Adjutant."

"Then at least temporarily mounted." Fingel went to the caravan door. "Sergeant-Major," he called, "have the men start digging out this trailer."

"Sir."

"You've left it rather late," I said to Fingel.

"Part of the plan . . ."

A party of HQ clerks started digging away one end of the hole, in order to form a ramp up which the caravan might be towed. Meanwhile some dim figures, all hung about with straps and packs and pouches, had appeared at the far end of the copse. "That's him," said Fingel, peering through a window. He opened the window and stuck his head out like a jack-in-the-box. "Hurry up, you chaps," he called to the diggers: "I want to get away before the Brigadier and his toadies come crawling round to spy on us." He shut the window with a snap. "That," he said to me, "was so that the Brigadier will think we haven't seen through his disguise and don't know he's here."

The Brigadier and his party advanced in a casual way and soon became absorbed into the mêlée of scurrying soldiery – not a difficult matter, as it was now almost pitch dark and no lights were allowed because of "security". After a few minutes, doubtless devoted to expert nosing, a high voice as of a Sealyham in season was heard: the Brigadier in person, complaining.

"Now," said Fingel: "signal your sergeant."

"Too-whit-too-whoo," I called and felt very foolish. But the agreed answer came back ("Too-whoo-too-whit") and within a few monents my anti-tank guns began to roll up out of the hollow. The Brigadier went on griping away at the edge of our hole, obsessed with his subject, heedless of all else.

"Slack, slovenly, incompetence," he yapped. "No effort, no method. Where is the officer in charge?"

"Here," said Fingel, marching up the ramp. "Who are you, interfering with my men?"

"I'm your Brigadier."

The Brigadier's staff began to gather behind him.

"No, you're not," said Fingel. "Our Brigadier is a very civil fellow. *He* doesn't squeal at people like a banshee."

My guns moved on, drawn by their armoured carriers; but no one had ears for them.

"Why aren't you digging?" yelped the Brigadier. "The officer should set the example." And then, at last taking in Fingel's dainty accoutrements through the darkness, "Why are you dressed like that?" he screeched at Fingel.

"Why are *you* dressed like *that*? Brigadiers don't dress like squaddies on punishment drill. Not *our* Brigadier, God bless him. You're an impostor."

And still the anti-tank guns rolled on across the copse, ignored by all in the excitement of the altercation. It began to rain, very suddenly and very hard.

"Right, S'arnt-Major," Fingel called.

The vehicle to tow Fingel's caravan backed towards the ramp, routing the Brigadier and scattering his staff. At the same time the anti-tank guns at last reached the far end of the copse, and the massive carriers smashed through the Land-Rovers (concealed, as Fingel had rightly calculated, behind a prominent clump of bushes) which had brought the sneaky entourage from Brigade HQ . . . all the officers from which, hearing the hideous grinding and stoving, now swam desperately through the almost solid rain towards their mangled vehicles.

"Your men won't stop, I hope," said Fingel, as we moved off in the caravan and swiftly skirted the wreckage.

"Oh no. I was very firm about that, as you told me. They'd be scared stiff of being left behind when the battalion moves out."

"Good. This rain is a real bonus," Fingel said; "I hadn't dared hope for that . . ."

"And of course," said Fingel to a crowd of admirers a day or two later, "they'll never know who did it or how it happened because they weren't paying any attention and by the time they'd assessed the damage the guns and the whole battalion were off into the night.

"Not only were the Brigadier's Land-Rovers unable to move an inch – and him fifteen miles from anywhere in the middle of the heath – but they weren't even any good to shelter in, because he's got this fad about fitness, and his own order forbids the use of hoods on Land-Rovers to stop us getting soft. He must be the only officer in his Brigade who obeys it, and I hope he feels the fitter for it now."

Fingel Adjutans

"Three quid a day," said Fingel; "it's the standard rate for full subalterns."

"What discount for cash?" I asked.

"None. Only cash is accepted."

"Special terms for old friends then?"

"Balls to that. I happen to know," said Fingel, "that you had a nice little win at Ludlow Races the other day, about which you have been keeping studiously quiet ever since. Hardly the behaviour of an old friend, would you say? Three quid *per diem*, old bean, and that's flat."

"Very well." I passed Fingel six quid (the filthiest I could find) across his desk. "From after duty Tuesday till reveille on Friday?"

"Done." Fingel reached for the Leave Book. "So what's your story?"

This conversation was taking place during the early summer of 1955. Our battalion, at present encamped in transit barracks in the West Midlands, was to embark for Kenya in seven days' time. Now, Army Council Instructions state very firmly that no one is to be allowed leave of absence, except in the most urgent cases of compassion, from a unit that is within ten days of embarking for foreign service. Or at least that's what they stated in 1955. But Captain Fingel, who was enjoying one of his periods of trial and error as our Adjutant, was disposed to accept as "compassionate" any case which could be supported by folding money. Three pounds a day for full Lieutenants (as I was then), a fiver for Captains, and a tenner for Majors; for even Field Officers required Exeats from the Adjutant (who supposedly issued them on the authority of the Colonel) if they wished to leave barracks while under orders to sail.

"What's your story?" Fingel repeated now. "I've got to enter *something* in the bloody book."

"Grandmother's funeral?"

"For Christ's sake."

"Father facing bankruptcy and suffering from delirium tremens?"

"We've got young Milne down for that."

"Younger sister being expelled from Convent School for dancing in dorm naked?"

"Why should I let you away for that?"

"As you very well know," I said, "you're letting me away for six quid."

"But your story's got to be plausible. I mean, if the Colonel or some other nosey-parker comes round and says, 'Where's Raven?', and I say, 'He's been allowed off on leave because his sister did a naked dance in her Convent', I'm going to look exceedingly silly."

"The point is," I said, "that she is being *expelled*. I am going home to soothe my parents in their sorrow and help them get the balance of the term's fees back from the Reverend Mother."

"It just doesn't have the right *feel*. Let's say . . ." Fingel thought for a moment. "Let's say your sister has got engaged to an errand-boy without telling anyone, and you're going home to horse-whip him for his presumption, your father being too senile to attempt the task."

"Sounds too dated, somehow."

"Yes. . . . What about a dangerous abortion?"

"Too near the knuckle."

"Don't be so faddy."

"It is my sister."

"You didn't mind her dancing about naked."

"That was different. Rather jolly. I don't want anything sordid."

"I've got it," said Fingel. "She's fallen so hopelessly in love with her gym mistress that she can't keep her grub down, and the psychiatrist says she needs her favourite brother to cry on."

"Too soppy," I said.

"They like something soppy; that's what 'compassion' is all about. Anyway," said Fingel, "it'll bloody well have to do. I'm much in demand just now. I'm letting Sergeants and Warrant Officers in on this racket, and there's a queue of them all down the corridor. So be a good bean and bugger off. 'Lieutenant Raven, S.,' " he said, writing in the Leave Book; " 'A/Duty Tue. to Rev. Fri. Sister . . . in moral crisis and needs brother's help and advice'."

"But that could cover anything," I said.

"It's meant to."

"Then why didn't you settle straight away for naked dancing? You could have rooked half the Sergeants' Mess rotten by now."

"Get lost, Gladys," said Fingel. "If you're a second late on Friday, I'll clap you in irons."

But when I returned on Friday, after a pleasant two days of losing my Ludlow winnings at Le Touquet, I found that Fingel was badly down on his tyre-pressure.

"Trouble," he told me. "The Pustule has gone and found out."

"The Pustule" was the Regimental sneak. A pimply and undernourished Major, heavily married to a scraggy yet philoprogenitive wife, he got his own back on the human race, and at the same time hoped to further his career, by sniffing out and then reporting "in the line of duty" the private and professional irregularities of his colleagues. He was particularly

41

fond of delating against carefree bachelors, and was to be observed darting in and out of the Colonel's Office, gnashing his false teeth gleefully, some four or five times every day.

"He was bound to find out," I said, "once the Sergeants were allowed in on the act. They've all got mouths as big as their bellies – you know that. This is what comes of greed."

"Any other helpful comments?"

"Has the Pustule told the Colonel yet?"

"Mercifully, no. The Colonel has been summoned to a special briefing at the War Office about how important it is to be kind to niggers when we get to Kenya. These days, I gather, we're only allowed to fire at them if they've positively cut our heads off first."

"How long with this briefing take?"

"I'm not quite sure. But I know there's a whole squad of experts waiting to nag at him in London. The Colonel is to be interviewed by three generals, two bishops, an ex-missionary and a prominent female socialist. *And* by a professor of comparative religion from Sheffield University."

"All of which will surely give you plenty of time to come to terms with the Pustule."

"But how? He's quite remorseless."

"Even the Pustule must have a weak spot somewhere. Perhaps," I suggested, "we could send him a false message saying his wife is pregnant again."

"No," said Fingel; "she only whelped the last one a fortnight ago. Anyway, what's the point of telling him that?"

"He'd want to see her. Since he's parked her with his mother in Cumberland until he gets back from Kenya, he'd have to get your permission to go up there on compassionate grounds – "

" – And I could refuse him unless he promised to shut up about my leave racket?"

"Something like that."

"Do you know," said Fingel, "you've given me an idea. He'd never believe that she's in the club again already, but I think I see what to do. . . ."

*"The next morning at the mess breakfast table the
Pustule was handed a telegram."*

The next morning at the mess breakfast table the Pustule was handed a telegram. He read it, went yellow, slobbered slightly into his cornflakes.

"Fingel," said the Pustule when he had recovered a bit, "a word with you, if you please."

"When I've finished my breakfast."

"Now."

"Well, if you really must," drawled Fingel.

He followed the Pustule out of the dining-room, winking at me as he went.

"It worked like a charm," Fingel told me later that morning. "That telegram I'd sent him purported to be from his mother in Cumberland, and it said 'MUCH DISTRESSED BY DOREEN'S CONDUCT STRANGE MEN LOCALLY COME AT ONCE LOVE MUMMY'."

"How did you know he called his mother 'mummy'?"

"It's the sort of thing the Pustule would do. Anyhow, 'mummy' must have been right, because it worked. He wouldn't let me see the telegram, but he wanted compassionate leave, he said, because something serious was wrong with his wife."

"So what did you say?"

"I said my rate for leave for Majors was fifteen sovs a day. It had been ten, I said, but now we were so close to embarkation I'd had to put it up."

"You bloody fool."

"Not at all. The wretched fellow was clearly desperate – you saw what he looked like at breakfast. And once he'd used my special service himself, do you see, he could never report me to the Colonel."

"He accepted your conditions?"

"On the spot. Two and a half days' leave he paid for, and here's seven and a half fivers to prove it. He had to change a cheque with the PRI – I wouldn't let him go until I'd got the crackly in my hot little hand."

"But surely," I said, "he *can't* have fallen for that telegram. The whole thing's ridiculous. That wife of his – she's never looked at another man, and no other man, even in Cumberland, would look at her. And anyway, since she dropped her last brat only two weeks ago. . . ."

"But that's just the point, old bean, old bean. Have you never heard of Post-Natal Stupromania?"

"No."

"Neither had anyone else – until yesterday."

"What on earth are you talking about?"

"Post-Natal Stupromania is a disease of my own invention. It consists, as I describe it, of an erotic frenzy which attacks some women a few days after they have given birth, the simple reason being that they want to make up for all those weeks of not doing it – though I've dressed that out in rather more dignified medical terms, like *Privatio Clitoris* and *Furor Jejuni Cunnis*. Ladies who suffer from it are also temporarily endowed with enormous physical strength, so that if they want a man they get him, even when they look like the back end of a hippo. 'In extreme cases, patients have been known to coerce even their own grandfathers' – or that's what the circular says."

"What circular?"

"The circular which the Pustule received yesterday evening. Signed by the Director of Army Medical Services, distributed by Order of the Army Council, and headed 'Confidential Warning for the Perusal of Married Personnel of All Ranks: Digest of Information concerning newly recognised illness, based on recent report of Royal College of Gynaecologists'. I made quite a good job of it, if I do say so myself."

"You faked up that circular – "

" – And ran it off my duplicator. And then made sure the Pustule got his copy in good time to read it before he went to bed. So that when he received that telegram this morning, about Doreen's goings-on, he was nicely softened up first."

"He'll soon find out there's nothing wrong with her. *And* guess what's happened."

"*And* do nothing about it because it would mean admitting to the Colonel that he used my Rent-a-Leave facilities."

For a little while I said nothing. Then,

"I suppose," I enquired, "that the Pustule was the only person to receive that circular?"

"Oh dear me, no. Even the Pustule has a friend or two, and he might have asked them what they thought about it; so in the interest of consistency I sent a copy to every married man in the battalion. It will be very amusing, as time goes on, to see what they all make of it, particularly the prospective fathers out in Kenya. Compassionate leave home from *there* will come very expensive, I'm afraid. . . ."

Fort Fingel

"Liaison and Intelligence," the Colonel announced. "We are required to provide one officer who will act as a kind of post office, passing any intelligence we may hear on to the Kenya Police and the Kenya Regiment, and *vice versa*. Any volunteers?"

Silence. This was notoriously the kind of job which led to hideous foul-ups, and besides none of us knew the ground. For we were newly arrived in Kenya, in the June of 1955. Our role was to flush the starving and desperate remnants of the Mau-Mau army out of their hidey-holes in the Aberdare jungle, and then to bring them in, alive, for detention and questioning. A delicate operation, in unfamiliar conditions, with the politicians both in Nairobi and in Westminster breathing heavily down our necks: no sane officer would go within a mile of intelligence duties here.

"It's a full-time job," the Colonel said, "and a very interesting time for somebody, I should hope." Worse and worse: in the British Army, as in ancient China, to wish anyone an "interesting time" is the most formidable curse in the vernacular. "The incumbent," said the Colonel, "will also be required to pursue independent investigations, and the post will therefore be on detachment from Battalion."

47

And then Fingel's eyes began to glint in the way I knew so well.

"Quarters, Colonel?" he inquired warily.

"A requisitioned farmhouse near Lake Naivasha. Formerly the property of a rich settler."

Fingel's eyes registered this factor like tabs going up on a cash till.

"And what sort of staff?"

"A corporal signaller, a clerk and a batman-driver." This was generous: Fingel sniffed. "A batman *and* a driver," the Colonel conceded.

"Done," said Fingel, "provided you put me in cash to engage a native cook and a house-boy. I'm told they come very cheap."

"You are a junior Captain," said the Colonel, showing some spirit at last, "not a Major-General."

"I'm the only officer here, sir, who will even look at this job."

Pause. Then, "You may engage an African house-boy, Fingel."

"*And* a cook, Colonel. After all, the chap who gives the best dinners gets the best intelligence."

"Then have your bloody cook. And that's an end of it."

"I think," said Fingel to the assembled officers, "that I shall call the place Fort Fingel . . ."

And so Fingel removed fifty-odd miles to the shores of Lake Naivasha and set himself up in his farmhouse as "coordinator of Jungle Intelligence (Aberdare Mountains)". Two weeks later I was sent to pay him a visit.

"The Colonel," I said, "is rather hurt because you haven't sent him any intelligence."

"I haven't heard any," said Fingel; "I've been far too busy settling in, old bean. Come and see."

Fingel had done himself proud. His chosen sleeping quarters and private bath-room were palatial, his dining-room-designate tall and nobly proportioned. His kitchen, presided over by an African cook who had once served in the Nairobi Club itself, contained a huge refrigerator which was crammed with, among other things, two sides of smoked salmon and a 32-ounce tin of Beluga caviar. His wine-room was cool and munificently stocked; and what he styled his Grand Salon would have housed with ease a Whig duchess's soirée. Only the so-called Operations Room was rather less than adequate, having barely enough space for the corporal signaller and his transmitter, and certainly none for Fingel.

"I'm afraid there was nowhere else left," said Fingel when I commented on this, "so I shall sit out on the verandah, and the chappie can always call me if ever I'm wanted."

"I see. And when do you start work? As I've told you, the Colonel's getting restive."

"All systems set to go from now on," said Fingel reassuringly; "so tonight I'm giving a little house-warming to let the local people know I'm in business. I hope you can stay for it."

The guests consisted of four loud settlers and their boozy wives, three uncommitted females of a certain age, and a Sergeant in the Kenya Regiment. He at least, I thought, might be there for purposes of liaison, but – "Name of Dalgety," said Fingel when I asked about him, "big name in these parts – big name and big money."

The relevance of this remark became clear immediately after dinner, when Fingel led the way into the Grand Salon and showed us all, with some pride, a long table immaculately appointed for roulette. The corporal signaller, in a dinner jacket, was sitting ready with a rake and stacks of neatly piled counters. The house-boy was presiding over a phalanx of bottles enough to refresh the party till Doomsday.

"Just in case anyone fancies a little flutter," said Fingel. "Two-shilling minimums. Buy your chips from the croupier – he can fix you up with blank cheque forms if you're short of cash."

As Fingel well knew, there is (or was then) nowhere in Kenya where gamey settlers could go gaming. There was an instant and strong response to his invitation, especially from the unattached women.

"I've been training that Corporal for a week," Fingel told

49

me on the side, "and he has the makings of a first-class croupier. But I shall take over myself if they start playing high."

Which, later on, they did. At four in the morning, as the last coup was called and the last bottle emptied, Fingel's bank was ahead by something over £400.

"Are you going to keep this up?" I said, as Fingel saw me to my room in the dawn.

"I hope so."

"And if the bank turns sour on you?"

"It seems I'm entitled to special funds," said Fingel, "for paying informers. The accounting system, as always in such circumstances, is crude. So you see, old bean, I have capital. Where did you suppose all that food and drink came from?"

After another month had passed I was again dispatched by the Colonel to remonstrate with Fingel.

"You've sent us nothing," I said.

"Much better that way, old bean. If I did find out any information, it would mean action, and action would mean trouble for all of us."

"Well, at least you could liaise with the Kenya Police a bit and make the right sort of noises. They tell us you've hardly made contact with them."

"The Kenya Police," said Fingel, "don't like the cut of my jib. And I don't want 'em here, nosing about. I'm running a bit near the rim, old bean, what with all this roulette and the rest of it. Some of those women that come actually tip the soldiery for their services, if you see what I mean. So no policemen in Casa Fingel, thank you all the same."

"Then you go and see them."

"You know how it is, old bean. The days slip by and somehow I never find the time."

A car drew up under Fingel's verandah. A large and bronze *bwana*-female swam out of it, displaying an acre of thigh as she did so, and grinned up at Fingel.

"There you are, you see," Fingel said. "Get yourself a drink in the Salon, Daphne," he called: "I'll be with you in two ticks."

"Look, Fingel," I said: "the Colonel says that if you don't come up with *something* in a very short time, he'll recall you to Battalion. Either you find us some intelligence, or you'll lose Casa Fingel."

"I thought he might say that sooner or later," said Fingel, "so I have a contingency plan ready. I'm going to say I've found an informer, and then invent some intelligence (Mau-Mau gangs at such and such a place, for example), and then say it came from him. *That* should keep you all happy."

"But if we start acting on fictitious intelligence, *anything* might happen."

"Rubbish," said Fingel. "Nothing at all will happen because there'll be nothing there to make it happen. You'll just draw a blank, and I shall simply say that you got there too late. Then my informer will come up with another location (which, by the way, will cost my special fund a good deal), and you'll be too late once again, and so on, and so on. All quite harmless but it'll keep the Colonel nice and busy, as that's what he seems to want. Now you be a good bean and leave me to cope with Daphne; and tell the Colonel that I'm working on a new line and I'll send him a red-hot report within two days . . ."

So for some weeks thereafter Platoons and Companies, and on occasion the entire Battalion, fagged round the Aberdare jungle hunting non-existent gangs of Mau-Mau in order that Fingel might stay in his Casa and prosper. How long he would be able to sustain his bluff I found a nice question for private conjecture; but alas, I was never to know the answer. For in the event, when Fingel was finally rumbled, it was not for disseminating false intelligence, nor even for keeping a disorderly house or promoting illicit roulette; it was for the mere dowdy misdemeanour of employing a servant who was a security risk. His much-vaunted chef from the Nairobi Club turned out to have been dismissed thence because one of his brothers had a history of minor political subversion. The Kenya Police, detesting Fingel and "the cut of his jib", had checked on the blacks in his establishment; Fingel, typically had not. A coordinator of Intelligence who omits to check his servants for security is not to be borne with. Fingel came back to us to be Assistant Motor Transport Officer (his very worst thing). Casa Fingel was wished by the Colonel on to some conscientious sycophant, who dismantled the roulette table and renamed the place after the GOC.

Fingel's Benefit

"The coffee is always cold," proclaimed Fingel to the assembled Mess Meeting, "the beer is always hot; the eggs hard, the toast soft, the tea thick, the wines thin, the salt damp, the meat dry, the soup sweet, the milk sour – "

" – Enough," cried the Mess Secretary, trembling violently. "Let's see if *you* can do better. I propose," he announced to the Meeting, "that Captain Fingel be appointed Food and Wines Member of the Mess Committee forthwith. Seconder, please."

"With pleasure," said the Commandant. "Fingel is always boasting of his gastronomic expertise. Let us have it put to the test."

"Thank you, sir. All in favour, please show," yelped the Mess Secretary.

All raised their hands, including (insolently) Fingel.

"I'll show them," he said to me later that day. "I regard it as a challenge, old bean. The food in the Officers' Mess at this Depot has been a squalid joke, all over the county, for the last ten years. Visiting generals writhe in agony and think they have developed ulcers after every meal; newly joined subalterns weep into their pillows all night long and write home to their mummies for tuck-boxes. I feel as if God himself had sent me to set the matter to rights. After all, it's time I did something positive for the Regiment – "

" – Amen to that," I said.

" – And reforming the food in this Mess wou'd be a major benefaction. Fingel," he apostrophised himself, "the man who turned the Depot Mess into a place fit for Lucullus to eat in."

"It'll be time enough for boasting," I said, "when you've actually done it."

"Ah, old bean, already Fingel has a plan."

It was the early summer of 1957, some three months after Fingel and I had both been posted home from Kenya to our Regimental Depot in the West Midlands, where we were responsible for training recruits. Since our Training Company was staffed with highly experienced Non-Commissioned Officers, it ran itself quite satisfactorily without any very active intervention from the two of us, who therefore spent most of our time on the excellent National Hunt courses that abound in that area. However, the onset of summer had brought an end of National Hunt racing; and since Fingel did not care so much for the Flat, and, unlike myself, did not care much for cricket, he had been compelled to cast about for other interests. At first he had gone in for the daughters of the local gentry; but as these, having marriage paramount in mind, had seen little future in being fingered by Fingel, he had achieved very little in that quarter, and now, bored and disgruntled, he had turned most of his attention to his stomach. The West Midlands, however rich in National Hunt courses, was (and still is) poor in restaurants. Fingel, fed up with driving many miles to eat bad food at high prices, had determined that he would henceforth seek his culinary pleasures where these could be most conveniently and economically purveyed to him – in our own Mess at the Depot. He had therefore dedicated himself to raising the deplorable standards which obtained there and had spent the last three weeks tormenting both the Mess Staff and the members of the Mess Committee with his demands for interesting or at least wholesome refreshment. Such demands had often been made before, and as often resisted; but

54

such was Fingel's pertinacity and power of insult that even the sluttish and obdurate crew who ran the Depot Mess had been somewhat discomposed – to the extent that they had decided to turn Fingel's spleen away from them by co-opting him in their own ranks and had at length contrived, as I have just related, to make him personally responsible for the Mess catering.

"Oh yes indeedy," Fingel repeated to me now: "Fingel has a plan."

"Might one ask what?"

"You wait and see, old bean; you just wait and see."

*   *   *   *   *   *

For several days the food in the Mess was as awful as ever. Then, about a week after Fingel's appointment, there was suddenly a luncheon of masterly conception and cookery: hot marrow on fried bread followed by chicken breasts in oyster sauce. An excellent dry vin blanc was served (without extra charge, Fingel informed us) and there was a choice of appetising and unfamiliar cheeses. Dinner that evening consisted of red caviar with blinis and sour cream, a delicate and boneless fish broth, and an expert blanquette of veal, all accompanied by a selection of several wines *gratis*; and luncheon the next day was distinguished by grilled lobsters. By this time the message was getting through: Fingel had worked some sort of miracle in the kitchen. Needless to say, some of the old guard at once began to complain of what they called "trumped-up foreign muck" and of the automatic service of wine ("who's going to pay in the end?"); but since Fingel firmly asserted that in providing this food and wine he was not overspending the sums allowed for the purpose, most of us were entirely content with the new state of affairs, though all were convinced that Fingel "couldn't possibly keep it up".

Yet keep it up he did. Gulls' eggs and asparagus in season, langoustines and Dublin Bay prawns, even, on two occasions, fresh foie gras – all these and other delicacies, as well as a series of classical main dishes (coq au vin, chicken Kiev, entrecôte Béarnaise, etc., etc.), appeared in carefully calculated and stimulating sequence for day after day, week after week. The food in our Mess became famous. Local and municipal notabilities, who had previously despised us as "the military" or "that crowd at the barracks", toadied shamelessly for invitations; visiting warlords, who had once choked at the notion of our Mess and had often put up at the nearby hotel instead, now arrived a day early and stayed two days longer than they needed to. By the time that the first month of Fingel's administration had gone out, and there had been, as he had promised us, no perceptible increase in our mess bills, Fingel had come to be regarded as a gastronome and dietician of genius and "Chez Fingel" (as the Mess Dining-Room was now called) was envied and marvelled at by soldiers from Whitehall to Edinburgh Castle.

But doubts still lurked in certain breasts, not least in mine. If no extra charge was being made on our mess bills, how was all this luxury being paid for? Fingel, when challenged on this point by the Commandant, said it was all done by intelligent planning and marketing and resourceful use of by-products and leftovers. "The French system, Brigadier," he said: "if you hear of a glut of something, you buy it up cheap – even if you have to get up at four in the morning to do so. And for the rest, waste not, want not. Don't chuck your bones away – use 'em to make soups and stock pots. Or if someone leaves a slice of meat on his plate, mince it up and pop it into a pâté." The Commandant, who like many of his kind enjoyed his food but was largely ignorant of how it was procured and processed, was only too ready to be convinced. But I knew better. For one thing, no amount of intelligent marketing or getting up at four in the morning could elicit, from any source, fresh foie gras and langoustines at a rate which our Mess could afford; and for another, even if French techniques of planning and contrivance could be held to explain the new quality of our cuisine, how on earth had Fingel taught our sour and grimy corporal cook to apply them? Before the advent of Fingel, the man had taken positive pride in the vileness of the food which he prepared for the "fuckin' officers". How had Fingel induced a change of heart in him, let alone educated him to his present level of performance?

"Very simple, old bean," said Fingel, when I finally insisted on an answer to these questions. "You find a highly qualified civilian chef . . . one who's had a spot of bother in London, let's say, and is happy to retreat to the provinces incognito for a bit . . . and you hand over the Mess kitchen to him. The corporal cook is happy stewing in his married quarter all day and never coming near the place; the other scullions on the role knuckle under to the new man, without asking any questions, provided you unofficially double their pay. The new man knows how to handle the marketing, to make special orders from London – or even from Paris and Strasbourg – and that's it."

"You've got a civilian chef in there?"

"Oh yes. I knew of one who's done a spell in chokey for violating an apprentice or two in a famous London hotel. He's very glad to have the job. And nobody's noticed he's there because nobody except me goes near the kitchen. That's why the food was in such a foul state when I took over."

"But how on earth do we pay for all this?"

"In all the circs, we get our man at cut rates."

"But even so, he and his food must cost a packet. How can the Mess conceivably find the money?"

"By courtesy of Sergeant Sweenie Mack."

"What ever *can* you mean?"

"As Second-in-Command of the Training Company," said Fingel, "you may just have noticed that Sergeant Mack has for some time, by an inspired appointment of my own, borne the title of NCO i/c Coordination of Training and Resources."

"Yes. I wondered what all that was about."

"It means," said Fingel, "that Sergeant Mack is the man responsible for seeing that the three platoons of recruits at present under training are provided with the correct equipment and then do whatever they are meant to be doing with it at any given time of the day. As Company Commander, I am too occupied with documentation and policy to supervise much actual training, while you, my 2 i/c, are too busy playing cricket four days a week. So the burden of the thing devolves on Sweenie Mack."

"I take a look now and then," I said.

"Yes. At the one platoon which happens to be training in barracks. Sweenie Mack always keeps one platoon in barracks in case the Commandant gets his monthly fit of conscience and wants to see some activity in train. But where are the other two platoons? As long as *something* is going on under your noses, it wouldn't occur to you or the Commandant to ask."

"Well, where are the other two platoons?"

"Doing odd jobs of a menial but not ill-paid kind all over the county. Everyone, from squire to scrap-metal dealer, occasionally wants a temporary labour force for something or other. The word has gone round: get in touch with Sweenie Mack at the barracks – he has between sixty and seventy good men and true (two platoons) available on request to shift or dig, to push or pull, to bury or erect, at reasonable rates – and no trouble over unions or insurance stamps. Of course, a certain deference must be paid to military convention, so a code is used: 'Sergeant Mack,' some potential employer will say, 'I have some ground which you might find suitable for manoeuvring or exercising your recruits.' 'Very public-spirited of you to assist us,' Mack will reply; 'when is your training area available?' 'From 0800 hours next Friday,' he will be told, 'until 1600 hours.' And then off go our two platoons, while you are still happily abed, for 'training' at the time and place allotted, and back they come at tea-time, while you are elegantly playing at bat and ball, having earned, say, a hundred quid for whatever they have done there. Mack gets ten per cent and the rest keeps our chef and kitchen going – and enables me to issue free wine. At the moment we are averaging an income of £400 a week and expenditure of £350. The favourable balance goes into a special private account of my own."

"But the recruits – haven't they smelt anything fishy?"

"Most of our recruits are very simple-minded. West Midland boys, whether of agricultural provenance or industrial, are not perceptive."

"They're not quite potty either."

"Ah. Mack has a genius for presenting whatever task they must undertake in a military guise and making it appear to be a branch of training. Shifting derelict machinery becomes 'An Exercise in Disposal of Heavy Stores, previous to the Retreat'. Digging deep holes is, of course, 'Training in Excavation of Earth Latrines, as required by Army Council Standards of Hygiene for the Tropics'. And so on."

"Some of the recruits must see through that. The potential officers, for example."

"Mack knows all about potential officers, old bean, having had so much to do with the finished article. Potential officers," said Fingel, "are sent off to the Depot Education Centre all day long for 'Courses of Tactical and Strategical Reading, in Preparation for Officer Candidature'. In fact they read whatever they fancy and they know a good thing when they see it. There'll be no trouble from *them*."

"There'll be trouble from somebody."

"No doubt," said Fingel: "we are all born to it. But meanwhile we enjoy a very passable table, as I think you will agree. *Carpe diem*, old bean, as the Latin chappie has it: 'reap the day'."

*　　*　　*　　*　　*　　*

But alas, *carpe diem*, or something very similar, was also the maxim of our brilliant chef. After he had "reaped" the two more complaisant of his soldier-assistants in the kitchen but been vigorously complained of for his attempt on the third, he had to be (a) sacked and (b) explained to the Commandant. Luckily Brigadier Arthur de Courcy Villiers-Clunbury-Pratt, though slow of thought, was a man of this world. Wisely deprecating the prospect of an official enquiry, he pacified the outraged kitchen boy by the award of two months' compassionate leave, posted Fingel and Sergeant Mack away on long and punitive courses at the School of Infantry, and gently required myself to direct the Training Company in a resumption of normal schedules. "We can't afford any more rows for a bit," said this excellent old gentleman, "so get the show ticking over properly again, Simon, and cut your cricket from four days a week to three . . . just for the next fortnight or so . . . there's a good chap."

Fingel's Penitence

Tactical Wing,
School of Infantry,
Warminster.
June 27, 1957

Dear Old Bean,

It's just too cruel. I realise that I had to be packed off from the Depot for a time after the row about the queer chef and the rest of it, and I realise too that some sort of penalty was in order, from the official point of view. But I thought that just being sent to the School of Infantry would be considered punishment enough in itself, and that once I was actually here I'd be put on a course for fat and cosy Company Commanders or something of the sort – after all, I *was* commanding Training Company at the Depot. But what has happened is savage beyond belief. I've been assigned to a course for *Platoon Commanders*. To refresh my knowledge and rehabilitate my physique, according to the Posting Order; in other words, to bash me about. Obviously the Brig at the Depot wants to give me a shaking-up – and after all those beautiful meals I provided. There's gratitude for you. Me, Fingel, Captain Fingel, all of twenty-eight years old, on a Platoon Commanders' Course, along with a lot of horrid little ticks who've just passed out of Sandhurst and some bumptious young negro bucks from places like Nigeria. All as keen as mustard, of course, and as fit as mustangs. I did have some hopes of a couple of full lieutenants who are joining with University commissions; at least, I thought, after three years of Cambridge they'll take the Army with a big pinch of snuff and be a bit short in the wind like me. But not on your nelly – no allies in that quarter. The ex-undergrads spend all their spare time on long training runs, "to catch up with the young 'uns" as one of them put it. They're as keen as any of the Sandhurst warts and twice as sycophantic to our abominable Instructors.

As for these, they've got the word all right, that Fingel's to be put through the mangle, and they're grinding away like Trojans. "At the double, Captain Fingel." "Say 'sir' when you address a Field Officer". "Thirty seconds late, Captain Fingel; take Orderly Officer for a week". "Captain Fingel, since you are on a Platoon Commanders' Course, your monthly credit for drinks in the Mess will be limited to that of a sub-altern" – a really vicious cut, that last, and delivered by the most abominable of them all, a rumbling red-coat from the Beds and Herts called Colonel Ferrers-Box, OBE. He has a bald head with little tufted spikes sticking out of it, long and very bandy legs, and a nose like the stem of a golf-tee. He is in charge of all the Platoon Commanders' courses, but since ours is the only one going on just now he spends his whole time sniffing round us like a neurotic truffling pig who might at any moment go rabid.

If Ferrers-Box wins the horror prize round here, a very close runner-up is Major Kitby of the Royal Marines, who is in charge of the section I'm in. Kitby is a sword-and-bible-cold-shower-and-three-rounds-in-the-ring specimen, straight out of Baden-Powell's *Scouting for Boys*, who hates, in ascending order, gambling, sex and intelligence. When I raised a Bridge four in the Mess one evening, Kitby came and broke it up because he'd overheard us agree on sixpence a hundred.

"Permitted stakes in the Mess are a farthing a hundred," he shouted (yes, shouted), "and even that is an accursed thing." But what really sends him up the drain-pipe is any kind of irony or evasion where military duty is in question. Yours truly discovered a sweat-saving path through a thick wood the other day – a path which Kitby didn't know existed. He was so put out that I'd saved the section from hacking its way through the undergrowth that he declared the path to be "mined" and made us start again and cut ourselves to ribbons on the brambles.

So here I am, listening to priggish lectures about Leadership and Officer Quality, or, worse still, clumping round assault courses in ammunition boots and full webbing equipment, for all the world as wretched as a recruit at our Depot. But Fingel is out for revenge, old bean; he is out to tarnish and corrupt. For Fingel is the fallen angel, the creeping serpent in this garden of military innocence and efficiency; and despite the rosy health and squawking enthusiasm of the subalterns, despite the pee-brained integrity of the staff, Fingel will find the rotten apple that is always lying *somewhere* around and will place it where it may most noxiously ferment in the smug and virtuous barrel. Meanwhile, I crouch in my damp and draughty room, among forbidden stores of whisky and champagne (imported in brave defiance of Ferrers-Box, OBE), plotting and peering. Already I think I see my way. More of this in my next.

Love from
Fingel.

School of Infantry,
Warminster.
July 2

Dear Old Bean,

Always something new, they say, out of Africa. You remember I said we had some blacks on this course from Ghana and the like? Well, I'm not keen on blacks as a rule – nothing to do with their colour, just their infernal conceit – but I've spotted a real winner in our section. A horrible uppity brute he is, straight off a coconut tree but full of socialist saws and progressive instances, dead true to the modern form in every way. So what's so special about him? Old bean, he has a perfect photographic memory – something I've often read about but never seen in action. Show this black a page of anything – French, Greek, calculus, *anything* – and for the next forty-eight hours he can reproduce it in writing down to the last iota subscript, and this though he hasn't the first idea what it is or what it's about. If it's in English or his own lingo, he can spout it off orally as well; but the great point is that if you get him to look at a diagram or a map or even a page of meaningless doodles, he can reproduce it down to the last little squiggle for up to two days after he last saw it.

Now this, along with his colour (for Anglo-African relations being the sensitive area they are, the authorities here can't afford the tiniest row with him or about him) makes him just what I need for my works of subversion. You see, I'm the only person who knows of his remarkable talent. Feeling lonely one evening, and finding that all the goody-goody Sandhurst boys had gone to bed, I saw him hanging about and hauled him into my room *faut de mieux* for a drop of my private juice, after four large glasses of which out it all came (about his photographic memory, I mean) in a great spate of mission-boy boasting. He'd kept it to himself till now, he said, because he was afraid we'd all think it was rather weird and might give him unfair advantages in tests and so on; and I had no trouble convincing him that he'd better go on keeping it quiet. But since I now knew his secret he let me test his claims for my own amusement – and I found them as good as gold. I showed him four pages of my breviary for five seconds each, and he wrote 'em out word for word the same time the next evening. So here I am, sitting on a prize asset: an asset, what's more, who'll do anything for me in return for a few slugs of Scotch whisky, which he is very partial to but cannot normally afford because his stingy Government in Africa has the great good sense to keep him very short of money.

Now my broad plan, old bean, is this. The most closely

guarded secret round here is the details of the big three-day exercise which we do down on Dartmoor next week. If Oozahunga (that's his heathen name) can get so much as sixty seconds alone with the plans, which are kept in Colonel Ferrers-Box's office, he can commit them to his miracle memory, charts, orders and all, and later disgorge them (in return for three promised bottles of Black & White) to yours truly, who will be then in a position to fuck the whole thing up, greatly to the discomfiture of Ferrers-Box, Kitby *et al*. The problem is to get Ouzou (the witty soubriquet which the Sandhurst contingent has devised for him) into Ferrers-Box's office for long enough to make with his magic eye-balls while Ferrers-Box himself is out of it – a bit of a pill, this, as the place is tightly locked whenever Ferrers-Box leaves it for so much as five minutes. However, Ouzou's privileges as a black will help us here. Ouzou, like all the Africans, is allowed access to his personal file (to see what Ferrers-Box and the rest are writing on it and to make sure he's not being "discriminated" against); so that gets him into Ferrers-Box's office easy enough, and once he's there it shouldn't be beyond your old chum's ingenuity to goad F-B out of it for a minute or two, by doing something rude or annoying like letting off a thunder-flogger in the corridor.

I'm sending Ouzou in tomorrow morning. If *that* goes off all right, we're set. Cunning old Fingel has already worked out the general principles involved in sabotaging the Dartmoor manoeuvre, and once he knows the exact arrangements, times, places, etc., which the staff are working by, he will concoct a final and precise scheme (which will almost certainly include further use of the egregious Oozahunga) for the total disruption of the affair and the ruinous humiliation of Ferrers-Box and his whole ghastly crew.

More news soon (I hope).

Love from

Fingel.

Old Bean,

Just a quickie, to say that Ouzou went in this a.m. and God was good to us. My tentative notion for distracting Ferrers-Box at the appropriate moment had been to fake a fire in the Staff Car Park under his window; but this wasn't necessary, as one of the clerks mercifully had an epileptic fit in the outer office. While Ferrers-Box was thrusting steel rulers between the wretched fellow's jaws, Ouzou got his peepers on the goodies for a clear two minutes.

He's now busy here in my room, guzzling up his three bottles of whisky and making an exact transcript of all the orders, logistical and tactical, for the Dartmoor exercise, and all the pretty diagrams, panoramas and what not that go with them. As soon as he's done, I can make a minute by minute and yard by yard analysis of the whole caboodle and work out exactly where and how Fingel must strike. More of this when I've done my homework.

Love from
Fingel.

LOVELY OLD BEAN,

God has surely delivered the enemy into my hand. The Dartmoor manoeuvre turns out to be a real swine – but ideal for my farce-making purposes.

Each section is to be dumped at some point on the perimeter of Dartmoor at dusk, and then has to make its way by compass over hill and dale and river and bog to a central RV on a Tor of granite, where we're all meant to arrive by 1 a.m. We shall then mount a night-attack in concert on a deserted farmhouse,

"*While Ferrers-Box was thrusting steel rulers between the fellow's jaws, Ouzou got his peepers on the goodies for a clear two minutes.*"

having taken which we shall be allowed a few minutes off for bed and breakfast inside it before setting off once more to carry out reconnaissance by day etc., etc., etc., but none of the rest of it matters because Fingel will have wrecked the whole thing long before then.

The authorities' plan is, you see, that each section, while *en route* to the RV at the Tor, will be commanded by a selected student and also attended by its own Instructor, who will give assistance in case of emergency and will clock up everyone's marks for guts, bearing, initiative and all the other grisly qualities which they try to foster round here. Colonel Ferrers-Box will be awaiting us at the Tor to issue orders for the attack on the farmhouse, and at this stage a new lot of students will be appointed to command the sections during the attack. After the attack is over yet another new lot of students will be put in command of the sections – just in time for Ferrers-Box's master-stroke, which is this: having told the new section commanders that they can stand their men down to snatch a bit of kip and eat their haversack rations for brekker, F-B will stage a counter-attack on the farmhouse, this to be carried out by a Company of local Territorials, who, of course, know the country like the back of their horny hands. The said Territorials will creep up by stealth armed with "flame-throwers", i.e. with garden hoses worked off portable water-tanks; and the idea, a real Ferrers-Box *spécialité de la maison*, is that they should drench all the exhausted students just as soon as they're flat out with their eyes shut, thus causing much grief and confusion and providing a searing test of guts, bearing, initiative, *et cetera*.

Now, old bean. According to the lists which Ouzou memorised, *our* section is to be commanded by Ouzou himself on the compass march; by some little pig from Sandhurst during the attack on the farmhouse; and *then* by yours sincerely, Fingel, who is thus destined as the man that has to cope when the local squaddies start flooding the snoring subalterns. But observe, dear bean, how very neatly, *with the benefit of my forbidden knowledge*, the whole shocking affair can be restaged:

Ouzou, bribed by the promise of much Scotch, will pretend to lose the way to the Tor but will find it again before Kitby has to interfere (which he will anyhow be reluctant to do for fear of upsetting temperamental black Ouzou); meanwhile, however, Ouzou will have taken us near the farmhouse (of which, of course, we know the exact location) that is later to be attacked and counter-attacked. This gives Fingel the chance to slip off in the dark to where the merry Terriers are making their preparations (their base was clearly marked on one of Ferrers-Box's secret maps) and to pose as a messenger come from Ferrers-Box to order slight changes in plan.

The Territorials accept Fingel as genuine, first because they see the Captain's pips on his shoulders, secondly because if he wasn't pukkha he wouldn't know about the plan at all, and thirdly because local yokels, however well they know their own country, know very little else. So Fingel now instructs them to fill their portable water-tanks with lubricant oil from the spare cans on the troop carriers that brought them across the moor earlier that day (an arrangement projected in F-B's Logistic Notes) and to turn their "flame-throwers", *not* into the parts of the farmhouse previously specified, but into the adjacent coach-house, which, as Fingel knows from one of F-B's Administrative Diagrams, is where the Instructors are to take their rest. "We're putting all the slackers in there, you see," Fingel will tell the Territorials; "that oil should give them a bit of a shine, ha ha, what?" After exhibiting such further artful and affable nonchalance as may be necessary, Fingel then leaves the Territorial base, doubles round to rejoin Ouzou and the section, and is all present and correct when the section arrives on the Tor. Awful Kitby has not noticed Fingel's absence (a) because Fingel is one of fifteen students all strung out on a moonless night (trust Ferrers-Box for that), and (b) because Ouzou tortures Kitby by waving the map battily about and making eccentric (if eventually correct) calculations as to the direction next to be followed.

So. Ferrers-Box orders the night-attack, the little pig from Sandhurst leads our section during it, the empty farmhouse is misleadingly announced to have been "taken", Fingel is appointed to command the section, and is then instructed, by foul Ferrers-Box or filthy Kitby, to bed the section down; after which F-B and Kitby go smirking off to the coach-house, relishing the misfortune in store for Fingel and his boys, and little knowing that they themselves are soon to be half-drowned in engine oil, which will pollute and well nigh asphyxiate them, rendering them and the other Instructors quite incapable of conducting the rest of the exercise.

Love from
Fingel.

The Depot,
Salop.
July 5

My dear Fingel,

Yours just received. A most amusing plan. But just a little chancy, dear? Do remember that a lot of the factors which are apparently going for you (e.g. boozy Ouzou and the pitch-black night) might perhaps change sides.

Love from
Simon.

School of Inf.
July 6

Dear Bean-O,

Don't be a damp condom. Night-ops are Fingel's Best Thing – remember how I smuggled us out of that cathouse in Nairobi when the Military Police raided the place.

We go down to Dartmoor tomorrow. . . .

Love from
Fingel.

*　　*　　*　　*　　*　　*

Old Bean,

Well now, where to begin?

We begin, I think, as indeed we shall end, with the ineffable
Oozahunga. The mistake I'd made at the very beginning was
to let him get at the whisky *before* he had completed his tran-
scripts of the orders, etc., which he had seen in Ferrers-Box's
office. To be fair, he did a very accurate job of most of it; but
by the time he was three-quarters down the first bottle he was
liable to boob somewhere, and indeed, as it turned out, he
had.

It was, like all the classic errors, a simple matter of trans-
position. According to Ouzou's transcript, you may remember,
he himself was to command our section on the compass march,
some whipper-snapper from Sandhurst was to command us
during the night-attack, and I was then to take over for the
rest period, when we were meant to be biffed by the Terriers.
In fact Ouzou was quite right about the attack but he'd in-
advertently switched the command for the two other events.
When it came to the point, *I* was put in charge for the compass
march, and he, Ouzou, for the rest period (what there was of it).
Which was, when I thought about it, a far more plausible Ferrers-
Box arrangement, as the night-march offered the maximum
likelihood of shaming discredit for the man in charge, which
was just what Ferrers-Box would wish for me.

But however that might be, the immediate problem was
this: as section commander I should now be very much under
Kitby's eye for the whole march and there was no chance at all
that I should be able to slip away to the Terrier base and give
my revised orders about the employment of the "flame-
throwers". Luckily (as I then thought) I had time to have a
quick word alone with Ouzou, who of course was the only
other person privy to my plan, and persuade *him* to be messenger
to the Terriers (though just how he was going to convince them

71

of his *bona fides* I was far from sure), an office which he under-
took in return for the immediate hand-over of the flask of
whisky I was carrying and the promise of more on tap later.
After that we started on our march across the soggy moor.
When it came to the stage at which I had to bend our route (in
order to get Ouzou within reasonable distance of the Territorial
base) Kitby gave me a malignant look, hoping for total failure,
but that was one of the happier moments of the night, as Ouzou
slunk off undetected and I had the pleasure of watching Kitby
writhe with disappointment when, after a bit of palaver with
the map, I got the section going in the right direction again.
So far, then, all had gone to plan; and when Ouzou at length
rejoined the rear of the section (again unnoticed save by me)
just before we reached the Tor, and gave me a broad African
grin, it seemed that we were well on the way to success. I had
no time to question Ouzou before the attack started, as I was
busy being "debriefed" about the march by Ferrers-Box, but
that great toothy leer of his must surely mean that all was well,
and I went into the assault a very happy soldier.

I should not have been so happy had I known what had
passed between Ouzou and the Terriers. As I have since
deduced from piecing things together, what happened was
roughly this:

Ouzou arrived at their base smelling of my whisky and
flashing his enormous gnashers, and was greeted by a pink-
faced Major who'd had twice the amount to drink that Ouzou
had. They got on together famously. Any doubt the Major had
about Ouzou's authority to change the orders on behalf of
Ferrers-Box was soon dispelled (a) by more whisky and (b) by
the grandoise badges of rank worn by Second Lieutenants in
Ouzou's potty native Army – not single pips, like our warts
have, but bloody great gold palm-trees which cover half the
shoulder. So this Major thought that Ouzou was some young
African tiger, at least a Colonel, on secondment, and listened
with deference when Ouzou told him what to do.

"You pour dat water right out of dose portable tanks, man,"
Ouzou said, "and fill dem up with petrol instead."

"Petrol, sir?" said the Major, for even he was a little daunted by this.

"Dat's what de man said. Dat stuff wot you put into dem lorry-machines," he said. "Dat stuff dat smell bad."

I should explain that Ouzou, like many Africans of recent emergence, is not mechanically minded. (It is one of their few endearing traits.) Ouzou drew no particular distinction between lubricating oil and fuel oil, between different types of fuel oil, between three-tonners and troop-carriers – he drew no distinctions of this banausic kind at all; and I had not had time, during the brief period I had to teach him his message, to press them upon him.

"But surely," said the Major, "Colonel Ferrers-Box doeshn't want ush to spray all his shubalterns with petrol? A bit dicey, you know."

"It ain't going to be sprayed on goddamn subalterns," Ouzou said. By which he meant, of course, that it was destined for Colonel Ferrers-Box and the Instructors. This, however, he could not reveal, and being at that moment distracted by the failure of my flask to yield any more whisky and by the kind offer of the Major's bottle, he forgot to add any further instructions whatever and *made no mention of the coach-house*. It was, as even in his state he began to realise, high time he left to rejoin the section, and after a manic swallow at the Major's bottle he did so.

The upshot was that the Major, on the strength of the little he had heard, understood first that there were now to be no subalterns in the farmhouse and secondly that his men were to spray the place, not with water but with petrol. Presumably, he thought in what was left of his mind, Ferrers-Box was getting up some last-minute dodge to add realism to the exercise (the farmhouse being War Department Property and in any case a mere shell). He did rather wish that jolly African Staff Officer had given more details, but then what could one expect of blacks, jolly they certainly were but not given to precision.

All this is what I did not know when I settled down in the farmhouse to await the arrival of the Terriers and the degradation of Ferrers-Box in the coach-house. Ouzou, who had been busy taking over command of the section and giving a lot of loud and unnecessary orders, had then refused information about his mission until treated to nine-tenths of the reserve whisky in my water-bottle . . . after which he was incapable of any communication other than, "They got the message, man, they got the message." But this, on the face of it, was fairly reassuring. Anyway, nothing to do now but wait. Managing to ignore the Ouzou noises and the Ouzou smells on my immediate right, I began to doze . . .

. . . And was woken by a thin, high upper-class voice, which trillingly announced,

"I say, chaps, there's a very odd smell, somebody turn on a torch."

In response to which, somebody (of course) lit a match, and the next moment we were all yelling and fighting our way into the open, Oozahunga (unharmed) being well in the van. The hullabaloo was heard in the coach-house and out stormed Ferrers-Box; while in the light of the now incandescent farm-house the Territorial Major and a number of his men were standing foolishly about, looking dubiously at the "flame-throwers" in their hands.

"What the devil's all this?" screamed Ferrers-Box at the Major.

For answer the Major pointed abjectly at Oozahunga, who in turn started to point at me. Luckily the din was still colossal, so –

" – You take the rap," I hissed at Oozahunga; "they'll let you off because you're a nig – because you're a foreigner and they won't want a production about it. I'll give you two cases of whisky."

"Twenty cases," said Ouzou, who was now stone sober. "This is mingi heap trouble for you, man."

"Ten cases."

"Fifteen, man."

"Done."

So Ouzou took the can – he's been a real brick about that

74

– with some tale about how he had stumbled on the Terrier base accidently and had thought up "one good-damn hooray jokey-jokey" in order to "take out de piss from all dem damn toffee-nosed boys from Sandhurst School". This admission has enabled the Commandant of Warminster to book him on to the slow boat for Hubba-Hubba or Beri-Beri or wherever, whither he will bear to his Government a diplomatic and propitiatory report which praises his "enthusiastic (if somewhat misapplied) sense of initiative" and mildly deprecates his part in causing the demise of two subalterns, who succumbed to incineration. As well as this report, Ouzou will take with him fifteen cases of Black & White whisky, the purchase of which, arranged with some difficulty from this hospital, has exhausted the funds I ran up for myself during Sergeant Mack's Training Coy bonanza earlier this summer.

On the debit side, then, I am badly burned on the botty and, once again, flat broke. On the credit side, however, I shall miss the rest of that intolerable course at Warminster, and I have been an incidental element in bringing about the premature resignations of loathsome Ferrers-Box and ferocious Kitby, both of whom are held to have been negligent in supervising the student career of Oozahunga. Just about worth it, on balance.

Love from
Fingel.

P.S.   I almost forgot – the two subalterns who went up with the farmhouse. These were the two graduates I told you of some time back who were commissioned direct from Cambridge. Both of them, it seems, were of Downing College and the Welch Regiment, so that's quite all right.

F.

Fingel's Heritage

"Good news," said Fingel. "I've just had a wire to say my mother's ill. They think she's really had it at last."

"What's in it for you?" I said.

"I split the winnings with my sister. The trouble is that *she's* a bitch if ever there was one. I wouldn't put it past her to get the will changed at the last minute and scoop the whole kitty herself. So I'd better push off to the death-bed p.d.q. to keep an eye on my interests. Good job I'm in England just now."

Fingel then departed on compassionate leave and was back three days later.

"Any luck?" I said, as I watched him unpack in his bedroom.

"She's been cured by one of those officious new drugs," said Fingel morosely. "I left her as fit as a crocodile in the zoo. And that's not the worst of it."

He took a bottle of whisky from his suitcase and poured a generous sextuple into his tooth-glass.

"My sister," he said: "she got there first and fielded her four children. Had 'em kneeling in rows by the bed praying for 'darling Granny'. That went down big with my mama, and for two pins she'd have sent for the lawyer to rub me out of her will there and then as a depraved and childless bachelor – her very words, old bean. But at the last second I managed to trump the trick by saying that I'd arranged a country cottage near here for her to come and convalesce in. Acute psychology, if I do say it myself. Loving prayers cost nothing, but here was *I* demonstrating my affection in an expensive and apparently optimistic manner. The only trouble was, mama called my bluff. As soon as I told her about the cottage, she was so bucked by the thought of getting something free of charge that she turned the corner, and inside twenty-four hours she was sitting up and eating like a hyena. My sister made the best of a bad job by wheeling her brood in to 'thank God that darling Granny's well again', and then slunk off home to wait for the next round. Meanwhile, I'm stuck with my offer. Unless there's a relapse, my mother will be here in a week yelling to see this rural retreat I've promised her."

"At least," I said, "your expectations are still unaffected. You haven't yet been crossed out of the will, and if you play the pasties carefully while your mother's down here, *you* could do the dirty on your sister and wind up with the jackpot."

"You haven't understood, old bean. You've never met my mother. My only hope of staying in her will at all is by steering clear of her altogether. She has fads, you see. One minute she's a vegetarian, the next she's a nudist, and anyone near her has got to toe the line *or else*. If she comes here and announces, for example, that she's going to join the Seventh Day Adventists, I'll have to join too or I'll be finished. I've only survived so long because I've almost always been abroad and she couldn't check up on me. I'd get a letter saying I'd got to go in for Yoga or Spiritualism or White Magic, and I'd write back from Africa or wherever saying 'yes, mummy dear', and there was an end of it. In theory, old bean, in the last six years I've become a Jew and a Moral Re-Armer and a Trotskyite and a Mormon and even, despite my profession, a Pacifist – none of which has been very bothersome because mama was never around to supervise. But now . . . if she comes here to recuperate. . . ."

"How much is she worth?"

"She could cut up for twenty thousand. Ten thou for Fingel, as the stakes are now apportioned. Not to be tossed away lightly."

"No. Have you actually found a cottage for her?"

"Of course not. I thought the thing up on the spur of the moment when I thought she was going to croak at any second."

"Well, in view of all you say, you'd better put her off."

"Can't. She's rearing to come. In a week at most, she says."

"In which case you'd better start looking," I said. "What's been the matter with her?"

"Pneumonia. She's always had a weak chest."

"You'll have your work cut out to find anything suitable for a delicate old lady round here."

Fingel took a long pull at his whisky.

"Do you know, old bean, the same thought has just occurred to me." For the first time since he had been back in barracks Fingel slowly began to smile. "I shall really have to be . . . *very* selective."

*   *   *   *   *   *

"I've found just the place for mummy," said Fingel three days later. "Clean, dry, sunny southern outlook, as pretty as a picture on a box of choccies. I had to pay a large deposit, in cash at that, but nothing's too good for my dear old mother."

"How very filial of you."

"Yes, isn't it? Only one thing worries me, old bean. The geyser in the bathroom is old fashioned and somewhat volatile in its behaviour."

"You'd better warn your mother about that."

"Yes, of course. Don't want her to go short of hot water. Now I've let myself in for this visit, I'm really going to take good care of her."

*   *   *   *   *   *

"She's coming tomorrow," said Fingel two days later; "bringing a chum for company."

79

"Is that good or bad?"

"Bad. The said chum's an old girl who lived near us during the war. So she knew me as a child, when I was even nastier than I am now, and she takes a low view of my moral character. She'll be very sharp at faulting Fingel, and she'll encourage mama to be likewise – not that she'll need much telling."

"They can't be too beastly to you, after you've taken the trouble to find this cottage."

"*And* paid for it."

"Precisely," I said. "That makes them your guests. They ought to be grateful."

"Gratitude, old bean, is not on their *agenda*. Anyway, they both regard me as if I was still in knickers. I used to skulk off to the local cinema when I was meant to be digging for victory in the garden. They've never let me forget it."

Fingel rang the bell for the Mess waiter.

"How do you propose to entertain them?" I asked.

"I'll play it by ear.... Brandy, please, Corporal; my measure for special occasions."

Fingel's measure for special occasions, good or bad but mostly the latter, was about two-thirds of a tumbler.

"Tomorrow," continued Fingel as the Mess Corporal went about his mission, "I'll meet 'em at the station and help 'em move in. Then dinner at The Royal George. I haven't got much further with my plans than that. Except," he said, "in one respect: I've had Sergeant Mack take a look at that geyser ... to make sure it'll come up to scratch."

"What does Mack know about geysers?"

"He once went on a vehicle fitter's course. He understands gas pressures."

"What did he say about this lot?"

"That they're very precarious . . . as I supposed. He's shown me how to control them."

"And you'll show your mother and her chum?"

"Oh yes. Tomorrow when I instal them. As I said the other day," mused Fingel, whisking his special measure from the

Mess Corporal's tray, "I'm really going to take care of her."

*   *   *   *   *   *

"Well?" I said the next evening, when Fingel had returned from dining his mother and her chum at The Royal George.

"Not well. Ghastly. Guess what the new fad is."

"Japanese Cinema?"

"Even more boring."

"Fidel Castro?"

"Even more of a bloody pest than he is."

"Equality for black immigrants?"

"No. Even more sickening than that."

"My imagination fails me."

"Teetotalism. In all the years we've never had that before. Never as bad as that. In fact, one of the few nice things about my mother was that she liked a drop or two. But now she says drink is the curse of humanity and she made me have water all through dinner."

He sobbed slightly and pressed the bell.

"What's the programme for tomorrow?"

"Mama's chum is going to cook us all dinner at the cottage. Woolton pie, to remind us of the war. Corporal, thank God you've come; the best brandy, three of my special measures. At the double, Corporal, left, right, left. . . . Old bean, I don't think I can bear it. I shan't even be able to tank myself up before I go, because if she smells alcohol on my breath I'll be out of her will like a cork out of a pop-gun. I hardly even dare to drink these now" – he snatched two of his special measures from the Mess Corporal's tray – "in case she's sneaked up here somehow and is peering through the window."

"Pull yourself together," I said. "You know perfectly well she's doing no such thing."

"Yes," said Fingel. He drained the first glass and caressed the second. "Yes," he said; "I was momentarily hysterical. I know perfectly well she's doing no such thing" – a look of sickly cunning spread over his face – "because I know exactly

81

what she *is* doing. Running a bath before she goes to bed. She always has her bath at eleven-fifteen at night. At this very moment, old bean, she'll be entering the bathroom and going up to that geyser. . . ."

*   *   *   *   *   *

"*Salop Evening News*," Fingel read out to me. "'FATAL EXPLOSION IN CLUNTON COTTAGE. This morning, at about 8.30 a.m., an elderly lady was killed by the explosion of a geyser in the bathroom of Wrekin Cottage, Clunton, near Salop. She was Miss Dora Boot-Bradbury, who was staying at the cottage with Mrs Zenobia Fingel, mother of Captain Fingel of Cawnpore Barracks, Salop. Mrs Fingel was on a visit to her son but has now returned home in consequence of the fatal accident to her companion. Captain Fingel, contacted at the barracks earlier today, said, 'It was a terrible tragedy. I am beside myself with sorrow'."

"It was and I am," said Fingel, putting down the paper. "It could have been my mother, you see. If she'd followed her usual habit of having a bath before going to bed last night, she'd have caught the bang that undid Dora this morning."

"What went wrong, Fingel?"

"I expect Sergeant Mack gave me incorrect instructions about that geyser. Or perhaps mama and Dora didn't understand what I told them about it."

"You know what I really mean, Fingel. What went wrong about your mother's bath-time? Why didn't she have her bath in the usual way last night?"

"Good question," said Fingel. "What I'd forgotten – I mean, what you are now forgetting – is that people who have just had pneumonia are very cautious about taking hot baths in case they overheat themselves and catch a chill or something. Or so my mother was telling me when I saw her on to her train this afternoon. 'Anyway,' she said, 'I didn't much trust that geyser, and I thought I'd let Dora have the first go.' "

"Does she blame you for what happened?"

82

"'Blame' isn't exactly the word. She's one of Dora's executors, old bean, and she's down in Dora's will for a clear twenty thou, she says, and she'll be into the lawyer's lair the minute he opens up tomorrow morning. So I suppose," said Fingel, pressing the bell, "that things could have turned out worse. At least I've packed mama off home after only one evening on water, and now there's double the money in the pot the next time I throw for it."

Pandora's Trunk

"Take a look at this," Fingel said.

"This" was a glossy book of highly coloured and highly obscene photographs, quite ingeniously done if you liked that kind of thing, with a commentary in one of those languages which puts little circles over "i" and "j" instead of dotting them.

"Where did you get it?" I enquired.

"From the owner of the Urania."

The Urania was Fingel's favourite and most long-suffering restaurant in Limassol.

"*He* got it," Fingel continued, "from a sailor on a Danish boat which plies from Copenhagen. It calls in here at Cyprus every two months or so. The Danes," he said heavily, "rather specialise in stuff like that."

"So one had heard." And so one had. The fact remained that one had never seen any of it before, or certainly not so luxuriously laid out and so lavish in intimate detail. "Stuff like that" was in those days (the early sixties) a very great rarity, at any rate on Cyprus. I turned the pages with relish – until suddenly the book was whisked from my hands and locked with a clang into Fingel's black tin trunk.

85

"It'll cost you a fiver," said Fingel, "if you want to look at it any more."

"You old *Jew.*"

"I'm going into business," said Fingel; "I'm an acting Major now, you know, and I've got to start thinking of my old age." He then explained further. It appeared that Alexopoulos, the owner of the Urania, maddened by Fingel's huge and unpaid account but otherwise well-disposed, had decided to put Fingel in the way of making some money. Alexopoulos would procure large supplies of rude books from his Danish connection and would sell them to Fingel (at a profit though of course on credit). Fingel in turn would set up as distributor within our battalion, a function which his present post as Field Officer i/c Welfare, Amenities and Entertainments would greatly facilitate. He would charge a price of between two and ten pounds sterling per book, fifty per cent being refundable, not in cash but in reductions on future purchases, if the book was returned to him in good order and within a week. In this way, the theory went, he would shortly acquire enough ready money to settle with Alexopoulos both for the books themselves and for the quantities of food and drink lately devoured at the Urania.

"And then of course," said Fingel, "I can start piling it up on my own account. There'll be a complete change of stock, in case anyone gets bored, every time that Dane docks with his ship."

"You do realise," I said, "that even the Cypriots have laws about pornography. Archbishop Makarios doesn't care for it."

"The Cypriot police won't trouble *us.*"

"You're also committing an offence under British Military Law: conspiring to corrupt the morals of Her Majesty's soldiers, or something of the sort."

"As a matter of fact," said Fingel, "I had just thought of that. So I'm going to keep all the goodies in here" – he rapped the black tin trunk – "and put the trunk itself into Welfare and Amenity Stores. RQMS Jameson's in charge of the Stores, and I'll make him sign. So if there should be trouble...."

"... It's on somebody else's signature. But who's going to hand the stuff out and collect the cash?"

"Ah," said Fingel: "who but Sergeant Mack?"

Sergeant Sweenie Mack was by now a very old familiar of Fingel's. Whenever Fingel was shunted on to a new job, Mack always contrived to follow him before long in some subordinate capacity and assist him in whatever enterprise was in train. True to form, Mack had recently joined Fingel's office as "Chief Clerk, Welfare and Amenity" and was doubtless eager to get his teeth into some such squalid task as Fingel was now proposing for him.

"Sweenie Mack will have a key to my trunk," Fingel now enlarged, "the only key there is apart from mine. He'll slip round the lines with three or four books at a time, explain the system, get it all going. So in fact, you see, personally I shan't have anything to do with it at all."

"What's Sweenie's cut?"

"Five per cent."

"Pretty manky."

"Yes. I caught him sniffing after one of the band-boys again, so he's in no position to bargain just now."

For three weeks or so (I gathered from Fingel) everything went very well. The black tin trunk, with Fingel's name now painted out and *Theatre Props (Amenities)* painted in on top of it, reposed safely in the Welfare and Amenity Stores in nominal charge of the RQMS. Sergeant Mack, as Chief Welfare Clerk, had the entrée to the Welfare Stores, which, being merely a distant and minor branch of the main Battalion Stores, were normally presided over by a genial dipsomaniac called Lance-Corporal Sphinck, whose supervisory efforts were minimal. Mack therefore had no difficulty in visiting the trunk with his key and obtaining or returning books whenever he wished. The market was good and the turnover brisk; for the district in which we were encamped offered little diversion to our troops and, as Fingel put it, "illustration assists imagination". Thus the project combined profit with benefaction, Fingel was speedily enabled to pay all his dues to Alexopoulos, and satisfactory negotiations were already under way for the purchase of a fresh consignment on the next appearance of the Dane – when suddenly disaster loomed, in a totally unexpected form and heralded by Sergeant Sweenie Mack, who arrived gibbering in Fingel's quarters one evening just as we were about to set out for a celebrative dinner at the Urania.

"Yon trunk, sir," said Sergeant Mack: "it's gone from the Welfare Stores."

"Gone?"

"Signed out, Your Honour."

"Signed out, Sergeant? By whom, for God's sake?"

"By the Colonel, sir. As Your Honour kens, there's to be a Fancy Dress Ball for the officers and their ladies at the Polo Club on Hallowe'en. So the Colonel comes enquiring at the Welfare Stores: 'Ma wifey's avid to wear something special for the Ball, Corporal Sphinck,' he says; 'have ye no some costumes for theatricals or the like?' Whereby that drunk loon Sphinck sohow stabs his paw through a mist of meths and shows the Colonel Your Honour's own trunk marked *Theatre Props*, and the Colonel asks for the key, and Sphinck says he knows of none, and the Colonel calls him a daft booby and orders the trunk taken to his quarters – 'Foreby we'll get it open somehow,' says he, 'and ma wifey can have her pick'."

"It's gone to the Colonel's house already?"

"Already, Your Honour."

"How many of those – er – books were there in it?"

"At least ten, sir, which weren't out the noo."

"Let us all keep quite calm," said Fingel. "All that is known of that trunk is that it was delivered to the Welfare Stores for safe keeping and was signed for by the RQMS, who is officially responsible for those Stores. No one is known to have had anything to do with the trunk since . . . unless Sphinck has spotted you getting at it, Sergeant Mack?"

"No, sir. Sphinck bides on his arse when I go there. And did he no tell Himself that he knew of no key?"

"So," said Fingel. "That trunk is simply a trunk marked *Theatre Props*, until recently on charge to the RQMS. And that is all."

"But how did you explain it to him when you got him to sign for it?" I asked. "He must have known it came from you."

"I told him it came on special distribution from the Education Corps – part of a scheme to encourage amateur dramatics."

"They'll soon explode that," I said. "Can't you see, Fingel? Your cover was perfectly sound if it had just been a case of some busybody reporting that those books were going round the place. No connection could ever have been established, as you rightly calculated, between them and that trunk or between them and you. But now the trunk itself has been seized . . . and the moment the Colonel gets it open and his 'wifey' gets a sight of those technicolour pudibunda flailing about, they're going to track that trunk back, inch by inch, to where it truly belongs, and they're going to wind up pointing at you."

"Och aye, Your Honour," said Mack, nudging Fingel fiercely in the navel, "the Captain here says sooth. At ilka cost we must stop the Colonel from opening that trunk."

"Sweet Jesus Christ," droned Fingel, "why must this happen just before dinner? Very well, Sergeant Mack: follow me. . . ."

*   *   *   *   *   *

"Really, you know, Sergeant Mack is getting to be a bit much," said Fingel, as we finally set off for the Urania an hour and a half later.

"I can't see that any of this is his fault. Anyway, what happened at the Colonel's?"

"Well" Sweenie and I drove to his house in the Land Rover, hoping it wasn't too late, and told him how sorry we were there was no key to the trunk, and that we'd come to take it off to the MT Workshops, where we'd open it up for him with one of those implement things they have and then bring it back. Desperation ploy, you see. Anyhow, it *was* too late. The

Colonel looked as grim as hell, and said his wife had already picked it open with a hairpin.

"'I hope she found something suitable for the Ball,' I said, meaning to bluff it out to the last.

"'She found something all right,' the Colonel said, and looked more savage than ever. So then I got ready for the worst, and began to marshal all my lies about how I had no idea what was in the trunk or how it got there – when suddenly there was a scream of 'Oh, Major Fingel, and what do you think of this?', and down the stairs came the Colonel's lady, all got up like La Goulue the Can-Can dancer, black net stockings and one of those dresses with a kind of rubbery hoop, that tilted up under her chin every two seconds and showed off acres of mottled thigh and a bunch of blue ribbons flapping about on her crotch. No wonder the Colonel looked so fierce. 'Isn't it amusing?' she trilled. 'Just what I fancy for the Ball. I'll go as a Loose Woman. Only as a joke, of course. But so *original*.'

"There was a funny strained look on Sergeant Mack's face, as if he didn't know whether to cry or to be sick, and as for me, all I could do was say sillily, 'So you found that in the trunk, did you?' 'Oh yes,' she squeals, 'and dozens more underneath, but I didn't bother with them because I knew this was *mine* the moment I saw it. It *must* win the prize. So daring.'

"'Then perhaps, mahm,' says Mack, choking on every word, 'ye wouldna mind if we took yon trunk away to the Welfare Stores again. You'll no want it cluttering up the hoose, I'm thinking.'

"'Yes, for God's sake take the damn thing away,' said the Colonel, and *sotto voce* to me, 'before she finds a Salome kit or something.'

"So we yanked the trunk down the stairs and out of the house, followed by Madame's happy laughter, and took it to my office. Inside it, sure enough, was a great pile of dresses, ranging from the Queen of the Amazons to the Indian Maiden, and underneath them all, safe and sound and undisturbed, was a layer of our porn."

"But where on earth," I said, "had the dresses come from?"

*"Down the stairs came the Colonel's lady, all got up
like La Goulue the Can-Can dancer."*

"Just what I said to Sweenie Mack. And then he started giggling and falling about, and out it all came. Along of his other little failings, Sweenie likes dressing up of an evening. But after I caught him chatting up that band-boy the other day, he'd realised that he was getting a bit too obvious, all ways round, and that others might take a less tolerant view than I did; so he decided to play it safe for a while, and among other precautions he hid all his dresses away in that trunk.

"'You degenerate little man,' I told him: 'Queen of the Amazons, indeed.'

"'But Your Honour minds,' he said, 'that had it not been for ma clobber, the Colonel's wifey would have got her eyes full with braw sweaty pubics and the rest; and for all she may dress a bit wild for that Ball, she'd have raised a great nasty blither about books full of red-hot naked lewdery.'

"And of course," said Fingel, "Sergeant Mack was quite right. His drag had saved the game. He's a bit worried," said Fingel as we drew up outside the Urania, "about getting that Can-Can outfit back safely. Though none of the band-boys go for it much, he says it works wonders with that straw-haired corporal in the Regimental Police."

Fingel on Tour

"Well," said Fingel, as we embarked on the *vaporetto* from the Casino Municipale, "that leaves us rather short of money."

"It leaves *you* rather short of money," I emended.

Fingel and I were driving back to England from Cyprus. Throughout the trip Fingel had been not only at his most outrageous but also at his most inept. On the Turkish boat from Famagusta to Mersin he had decorated a bust of Ataturk with a pair of horns crudely contrived from bananas. Amid the ruins at Ephesus he had pretended to be my attendant eunuch and pimp, mincing, leering and nudging whenever anyone of either sex and under seventy came past us.

Although his behaviour had improved a little in Greece, there had been an ugly scene at Delphi, where he tried to sell an American lady "her own personalised oracle" for 1000 drachmai. And now, as we were pausing in Venice, he had gone and lost every penny he possessed in the casino. It was really too much. By 1962, when all this was happening, Fingel had been promoted a substantive Major (by grace of Beelzebub) and was too old, I considered to continue as *enfant terrible* of the regiment. Fingel must be brought to book.

93

"*You* are rather short of money," I repeated now. "In fact you have none whatever. Whereas *I* have enough to get home in comfort."

"No you haven't. It's my car."

"There are trains."

"You couldn't desert me," Fingel wheedled.

"With equanimity. But I shan't . . . yet. Now then. I shall have to pay your hotel bill here in Venice," I said, "and I shall have to pay for all the petrol for the rest of our journey. That means there must be very strict economies in other matters – all of which will be borne by you."

I then outlined my scheme. I would graciously condescend to rescue Fingel and continue with him in his car, but he must understand that thenceforth he was on a subsistence allowance of thirty shillings a day. How he spent it – on food, on board, or on bawdry if he could get it – was his affair, but thirty bob *per diem* was his lot.

"Right," said Fingel. "A week to go between here and Dover; that's ten guineas, I make it. Hand it over."

"No," I said. "I shall hold the purse. Your allowance will be payable daily at noon."

The next day I paid the sums required to get ourselves and the car quit of Venice. These were substantial, as Fingel had had four bottles of whisky put on his hotel bill and the garage in the Piazzale Roma charged double the advertised rate for parking, apparently on the ground that we were leaving on the eve of a saint's day. We then set off for the Brenner Pass, and at noon I gave Fingel his thirty shillings (2400 lire in those days) almost all of which he immediately spent on lunch. Towards evening, pondering spitefully on what Fingel was going to do about dinner and a bed, I fell asleep in the car, and woke to find that we had left the main road and were circling up a side road into the hills above.

"Where the hell are we going?" I said.

"Quarters for the night, old bean. There should be a clearing in this wood somewhere . . . yes, this will do nicely. *Most* economic. To bed with the sun and up with the lark. We shall

*"Amid the ruins of Ephesus he had pretended to be my
attendant pimp."*

sleep in Nature's bedchamber. 'Blow, blow, thou winter wind, thou art not so . . .'."

"Shut up," I said. "How are we to sleep up here without freezing to death?"

"I don't know about you, but *I* have an operational sleeping bag in the boot which the QM passed on to me cheap."

"Food and drink?"

"*I* have some prawns, some salami sausage and some Parma ham, which I thoughtfully purchased while you were having a pee after lunch. Just enough for one, I'm afraid: I couldn't afford more on my allowance. I also have an individual tin of self-heating soup, which I scrounged from my Colour-Sergeant, and half a bottle left of that whisky from the hotel."

"I paid for that whisky," I said.

"You shall have some, old bean, if you make yourself agreeable. But more than that I fear I cannot do for you, and as for a bed . . ."

"All right, Fingel," I said. "I'll stand you dinner and a hotel room."

"That's my bean," Fingel said. And later as we drove on through the evening, "I didn't really have any of those things, you know – except the whisky." And later still: "Hotels are rather scarce in these mountains. But I think this one looks quite suitable." With which observation, he stopped before the entrance of a five-star Spa hotel called the Excelsior e Balmoral.

"Very cosy, these Spa hotels," Fingel said. "The staff are always trained to be especially considerate."

By the next morning we had had nearly £30 worth of consideration. "Look here," I said to Fingel as we drove on our way, "this cannot go on. I cannot pay out at this rate for both of us. You *agreed* to accept thirty bob a day in return for . . ."

"Yes, yes," said Fingel. "I'll be good from now on. Now cheer up, and try to spot somewhere decent for lunch."

"Lunch can wait till after the Brenner."

Fingel digested this remark. A few miles further on: "I've been thinking," he said: "those gold cuff-links of yours . . ."

"No. They were a twenty-first birthday present from my grandmother."

"I understand, old bean," Fingel said. "I had a granny too."

"I don't doubt it."

"She gave me a gold cross, which I always wear round my neck." He unbuttoned his shirt with one hand, flicked out a cross on a chain, fondled it for a moment, then returned it to his bosom. "I couldn't bear to part with it. So I understand about your cuff-links. Just give me thirty bob a day, and I'll be good. Dear old Granny, how I wish she'd lived to see me a Major."

Fingel sniffed, *in memoriam*. There was a wailing noise from the engine and the car stopped, luckily in a village where there was a garage thirty yards away. Fingel looked under the bonnet.

"The cranker-blippet," I understood Fingel to say.

"The what?"

"Serious, I'm afraid. I'll get a man from that garage. You have a drink in that café, and I'll fetch you when she's mended."

Touched by such consideration but apprehensive about what the repairs would cost and whether they would even be possible, I went into the café. An hour later Fingel appeared, looking very glum. God, I thought, the car's kaput. However, "All fixed," said Fingel morosely; "*en voiture*".

Such was my relief that I did not think to inquire how Fingel had paid the garage. After a while: "Small things, cranker-blippits," said Fingel miserably, "but very expensive to replace." He sighed quietly. "I got them to take Granny's cross in exchange I hope she understands, wherever she is. With only thirty bob a day I had no choice. . . ."

So of course I had to match Fingel's sacrifice and sell my cuff-links. We passed some pleasant days on the proceeds between Munich and Dover, with Fingel more charming than I had ever known him. Just outside Dover the car made a wailing noise and stopped. Fingel switched off, switched on, and drove on, shaking with laughter, and then repeated the performance.

"It's a little trick with the accelerator and the clutch," he explained; a Fingel seduction speciality, much more convincing with girls than that old gag of running out of petrol."

"There was nothing the matter with the car . . . *you never parted with your gold cross.*"

"Gold my arse," said Fingel; "it was something Granny picked up at a church bazaar – quite literally, I wouldn't wonder. But never mind, old bean. I'll pay you back what you spent on me. Cheque post-dated to next September, how about that?" Fingel laughed and laughed. "Cranker-blippit, indeed. Did you ever do an MT course? Just a little trick with the clutch. Watch."

He pressed the clutch in about half-way and stamped hard on the accelerator. There was the well-known wailing, then a keening, then a horrible squeal. The car stopped, this time in earnest, and luckily near the bus stop by the entrance to the Castle. I got out and took my case from the boot. Fingel followed me to the bus stop.

"I've got to be in London tonight, old bean. There's this girl who's putting me up. You will sock me my ticket? Or at least a bus fare into Dover? Old bean, I've spent my last ha'penny on duty-free booze for this girl."

As the bus drew up it began to rain. Since fares were taken by the driver at the door, fareless Fingel could not get on.

"There's a large garage at the bottom of the hill," I called. "No doubt they understand cranker-blippits, but they may not understand post-dated cheques."

Fingerella

"I am not going to produce a pantomime," declared Fingel, "and that's flat."

"But we've got to amuse the men over Christmas," said the Second in Command of the battalion. "Nothing for them to do in this bloody desert except drink themselves silly."

"A perfectly satisfactory way of passing the time."

"But the new Brigadier says we mustn't allow it. The new Brigadier says it's bad for health and morale. The *new Brigadier* says that it is the duty of the Officers and Sergeants to provide constructive and wholesome entertainments."

"It's the sort of thing Brigadiers are obliged to say for the record. They don't really expect any sane man to take any notice."

"On Boxing Day," said the Second in Command desperately, "the Brigadier is going to visit this battalion in this camp. Since he once served for a time with this Regiment, he will be doubly critical. After lunch, he says, he wishes to attend whatever entertainment we have arranged for the troops. For Boxing Day, the Colonel has decided, a pantomime will be the most appropriate; and he has therefore ordered me to get up a pantomime."

"Then get it up," said Fingel, "and the best of Thespian luck to you."

"I am appointing you, Major Fingel, to produce and direct it. I call Raven here to witness. If you refuse," said the Second in Command, "I shall have no choice but to inform the Colonel of the fact, hitherto charitably concealed from him, that the Mess now holds unpaid bills of yours which go back to July and also three cheques marked Refer To – "

" – All right," said Fingel; "I yield to blackmail. But why pick on me for this pantomime?"

"Because I am reliably informed that you have produced one before."

"But that was donkeys' years ago. Right back in Korea."

"I'm told it was a great success."

"Are you indeed? Did anyone tell you," said Fingel with a funny look in his eyes, "what that pantomime was about?"

"It was a version of Cinderella. My informant had read a report of it in an old number of the Regimental Journal."

"I see. I take it," said Fingel, "that since time is short you'd have no objection to my putting on the same show again?"

"None at all. Very few men at present in the battalion can possibly have seen it."

"Very well," said Fingel, the look in his eye now hovering near madness, "you're on."

*　　　*　　　*　　　*　　　*　　　*

"Of course," Fingel said to me later in our quarters, "no one remembers that old show now. It was only a Company affair, scratched up when we were out on detachment, and the so-called report in the Regimental Journal was just a couple of lines in 'B Coy Notes'; 'On Christmas Eve Second Lieutenant Fingel put on an hilarious production of Cinderella which was much enjoyed by one and all' – the usual hearty nonsense which the Company Commander thought suitable for official consumption. Well, 'hilarious' it certainly was . . . and a great deal else besides. Long before your time, of course."

"Please tell . . ."

. . . I'd been with the battalion in Korea about three months [Fingel said] and I was still junior subaltern, commanding a rifle platoon in B Coy. That October, B Coy had been sent off nearly 100 miles from Battalion to guard a ruined temple in the middle of the forest – God knows why, it was well behind our lines and of no tactical value – and we were still there at Christmas. By which time we really needed some fun, I can tell you. And of course the men were so bored that they were ready to join in anything which anyone suggested.

Well, our Company Commander – the chap responsible for that gushing note in the journal – was a sporty, gourmandising, gambly sort of a number called Geoffrey Ham. Easygoing and pear-shaped, the kind we don't seem to have any more. One day about a fortnight before Christmas Geoffrey sent for me and said,

'Look here, Fingel, we're going to be stuck in this hole over bloody Christmas, *and* a lot longer from what I can make out, and we're going to need something to live for. So we'll have a Christmas Panto. Cinderella.'

'Very nice too,' I said, 'as casual entertainment, but I don't quite see that Cinderella makes something to live for.'

'You'll see,' said Geoffrey; 'if the thing goes right, you'll see what I mean later. Meanwhile, I want you to produce it.'

So I said I hadn't the first idea how to begin, and he said not to worry, he'd be writing the script himself and masterminding the whole affair, but he wanted me as front man.

'You're younger,' he said; 'they'll like it better if you seem to be running it. And your first job is the casting – or rather going round to tell 'em all what parts they're playing. I've got the list here.'

The cast list had no surprises about it, just the usual kind of jokes. Geoffrey himself was going to be Baron Stonybroke and the two beefiest Sergeants were going to be the ugly sisters. One of the Company buglers – a jolly, rather spotty lad on loan from the Band – was going to be Buttons. The Sergeant-Major was down as Dandini with the Senior Lieutenant as the Prince.

The Company slag was to play the Bad Fairy . . . and so on and so forth. I myself was billed as Cinderella, which I didn't much fancy at first, but as Geoffrey said, *somebody* had to do it.

When I went round with the cast list, no one was very interested, but they all agreed 'to give it a go', it would make things a lot more like Christmas.

'How are we going to manage about your pumpkin turning into a coach?' said the Colour Sergeant (a knock-kneed beanpole who'd been cast as the Good Fairy).

'We'll discuss all that,' I said, 'when we have the first read through the script.'

'Can I see a copy now, sir?'

'No,' I said, acting on Geoffrey's instructions; 'they're not ready yet.'

I hadn't seen a copy myself, as it happened, and indeed Geoffrey wouldn't let anybody get near one until a few minutes before the read-through, when he handed me a pile to dish out.

'Tell 'em, if they get any ideas of their own we'll try to fit 'em in,' Geoffrey said.

Then off we went to the read-through in the NAAFI tent, before I'd even had time to glance at what Geoffrey had written, so that what was in those scripts was as big a surprise to me, when we all got started, as it was to everybody else. Mind you, I'd expected a few filthy jokes, and even a bit of camp, because pantomime carries a traditional licence for transvestite humour; but I hadn't at all expected the startling mixture of simple soldiers' bawdry and polymath eroticism which Geoffrey had concocted – and for which, of course, everyone else thought I was responsible, since I was supposed to be getting the thing up. They all began giving me most peculiar looks before we were past the first page of Scene I.

This features Baron Stonybroke working on his whacky accounts and explaining to the audience that if he didn't get one of his daughters off with a rich man pretty damn quick he'd be done for. Nothing out of the way in that. But he then went into a grotesque song and mime routine, from which it emerged that the two older sisters bribed spotty Buttons threepence a

"*I myself was billed as Cinderella, which I
didn't much fancy at first.*"

time to amuse them with his tongue in the woodshed, and that when this wasn't happening they conducted an incestuous sapphic relationship, using a vegetable marrow as a two-way dildo. All this has spoiled them for the marriage market, because

> Elsie's quim is now so wide
> You can drive a truck inside

(a typical example of the element of straight obscenity)

> And Buttons' fertile tongue,
>   Roving round her arcana
> Has made Doris over-hung
>   With a clitoral banana

(a fair instance of Geoffrey's more elaborate notions).

This, the Baron goes on, means that only Cinderella is left to save the old home by a wealthy marriage, but the trouble is that Cinders (or Fingers) is interested only in herself:

> Oh Fingerella,
> She cooks her own paella,
> Won't give the boys a sniff of it,
> A teeny little whiff of it,
> Oh, isn't she cruel-la?

So what, the Baron concludes, is to be done?

Enter now, Cinderella, who goes straight into the following ditty:

> 'Who wants cocks?
> They give you the pox.
> They put you in the club.
> Much better have a nice safe rub
> With your fingers
> That lingers . . .

Oh frotting
It's topping,
Oh frigging
It's for digging,
Oh wanking
It's so spanking,
 You never want to stop.

'But if you need a little variation,
Here's a tip or two for modish masturbation:

'A garden hose,
 The parson's nose,
  The gear of a car;
A spoon or a fork
 Or a burgundy cork

Will keep you quite happy
For hour after hour.

'So. . . .

'Who wants pricks?
They put you in a fix,
Give you far fewer kicks
Than a nice long nail
Or a cricket bail . . .'

Et cetera, et cetera [Fingel said] and so the caper goes on.
The basic theme is the frantic efforts of the Baron and others
to convert Fingerella from self-abuse to almost any other form
of sexual activity, in the hope of making her some sort of candi-
date for marriage with the Prince. He too has his peculiarities,
one of which is an obsession with anuses; and when the Baron
discovers this (in the Gents at the Ball) he hits on the scheme
of getting Buttons to tickle Fingers' behind while she's busy in
front, thus inducing in her a new taste which goes far to

105

accommodate those of the Prince and brings the piece to a happy ending. There are a number of sub-plots . . . such as the stratagems used to steal away the ugly sisters' vegetable marrow from the commode in which they keep it so that the Good Fairy can turn it into a coach. There is also much play with the Prince's embarrassment, while he is disguised as Dandini, at being presented with a consignment, intended for the latter, of dirty socks from the barracks.

And so, old bean [Fingel said], here was this outrageous script, and here was a tentful of soldiers who were reading it aloud and for the first time. As I've told you already, I was on the receiving end of some pretty odd looks from the very beginning, and by the time the ugly sisters arrived at the Ball singing,

> 'Ta-ra-da-bum-de-a,
> Who'll lick our labi-a?'

the men were positively goggling at me. I was getting very jittery, I can tell you. Had Geoffrey gone too far? Because you know how it is with soldiers: on the face of it nothing's too rude for them, but every now and then, for no very clear reason, they'll have a sudden fit of lower-class prudery and turn as prim as nuns. You can never be sure what may not set it off – probably something which you and I would find absolutely innocuous and something a great deal less disgusting than what they've been laughing at two minutes before. So it seemed to me that at any moment somebody was bound to be offended by something in Geoffrey's highly catholic repertoire – and then watch out for trouble.

But none came. There was a lot of bungling and hesitation, to be sure, but this was due to lack of practice at reading aloud. Nobody dried up in protest or disapproval. Although some of the cast were slow to grasp the more abstruse references, they were not at all put out when they grasped them. The truth of the matter, as I realised a little later and as Geoffrey had known at the outset, was that after what seemed an age in the middle of nowhere they were ready to accept and to welcome anything which promised a change; and that furthermore, any moral scruples which they might have had were lulled by a sense that they were now totally cut off, that they were somehow beyond space and beyond time, in a sort of no man's land *where nothing really counted*, where anything could be done or said with absolute impunity. For weeks this feeling of unreality and irresponsibility had been stealing up on them; and now here at last was this pantomime, written by one of their officers (me, as they imagined) and evidently countenanced by their Company Commander, to confirm them in their instinct. The looks which I had been getting were not of surprise or distaste; they were looks of complicity . . . looks of assessment. Geoffrey had not lacked reason when he put me up as the inventor of it all; for the fact that it was supposedly written by a very young officer, rather appetising (though I say is myself) and hitherto presumed innocent, gave it additional flavour, headier spice.

All this I began to understand when the reading finished. For a few moments there was complete silence. Then the bugler who was to play Buttons came across to me with a great grin on his spotty but amiable face and said:

'We'd better start practising, sir, hadn't we?'

This remark was greeted by general and genial laughter, led by Geoffrey. People now formed little groups, discussing the interpretation of their parts, thinking up refinements of humour and lewdness, devising ways round technical difficulties. The transformation scene and Fingerella's coach? Deck up one of the jeeps and conceal it under a camouflage net until it was needed. And so on. All was contrivance and good will. 'We're all going to have a lot of fun out of this,' the Sergeant-Major said; 'we're really going to live our parts, I can see that already.'

And live our parts we did. Almost overnight, reality for us became *Fingerella* and *Fingerella* became reality. We were not soldiers rehearsing for a pantomine; we were pantomime artists who were compelled to soldier. And soon it had gone farther: we *were* the creatures of the pantomime. Whether on stage or off, we existed almost wholly in the characters we were alloted for the play, we addressed each other and behaved to each other in terms of the world of *Fingerella*. Those who were not in the show, our audience, accepted us in our roles and treated us accordingly, so that before long the whole Company became a theatre, the players being distinguished but not alienated from the rest, both parties recognising and responding to the needs of the other. We, the players, required and received privilege and applause; our audience required and received a sense of authorised and indemnified Saturnalia. Geoffrey was now addressed by all ranks as 'Baron', myself as 'Fingers', the Sergeant-Major as 'Dandini', *et al.*, *et al.* Even as we gave our orders we clowned and sang and pranced and postured as our new avatars would have us; and yet in all essentials we were still obeyed, for Festival could not extend, it was tacitly understood, to military breakdown.

This alone provided, liberation was entire. Before long we sampled the erotic entertainments and connections suggested by the script, while the audience eagerly followed and improvised on our example. By the time the day came for the actual performance, the Company was a huge party of sylvan pleasure, with few abstainers and those tolerant. The performance itself was rendered with total naturalism down to the most intimate detail (*mutandis* in physiological areas duly *mutatis*) and was succeeded by a public orgy. Myself [said Fingel] I've always gone in for the girls, but I still remember with delight the ministrations of that merry little bugler, to say nothing of the other attentions which Fingerella naturally attracted. The Senior Lieutenant, as became his role of Prince, was particularly assiduous and turned out to have some quite surprising talents. . . .

But just as this state of affairs had emerged and flourished only because we were so completly cut off in our own artificial world, so it came to a necessary and automatic end as soon as we were called back to Battalion. No one needed to make a special point of it or give explicit orders; we all knew it must finish from the moment we left that temple in the forest. On the morning we mustered for departure, everyone was 'Sergeant' or 'Sir' or 'Private So-and-So' again; and although I have reason to suppose that one or two liaisons that had been formed were carried on in a cautious and vestigial fashion for a few months after we returned to real life, the party was over and by common consent of the revellers was consigned to oblivion for ever.

*　　*　　*　　*　　*　　*

"And so that," said Fingel, "is the reality behind that note in the Journal. *That* is at the bottom of my reputation as a producer of pantomimes. It certainly went with a swing – but not at all in the way the Second in Command thinks. And then of course, it wasn't really my baby. Geoffrey Ham was 'the onlie begetter' of that little masterpiece."

"What happened to him?"

"A couple of minor staff appointments, then retirement. But I've still got a copy of the script in my tin trunk."

"You're not seriously thinking of putting it on here?"

"I have the Second in Command's permission. You heard him give it to me – after he had specifically called on you to witness the conversation."

"He didn't know what he was agreeing to."

"Then he should have made further enquiries instead of just foisting the job off on me. He was bloody well asking for trouble. I shall enjoy watching his face while the Brigadier gets an earful of that lot."

"You'll never get the thing off the ground," I said. "The last time you did that show was with a Company of men driven half potty by boredom in the middle of the Korean forest. As you said, they'd been cut off from everything and everybody for so long that they thought anything they did just didn't count any more. Hence . . . those rather extraordinary side-effects."

"Well, in our case we have all been driven half potty by boredom in the middle of the Arabian desert. *We've* been cut off for long enough. A good many chaps may feel that anything they do here 'just doesn't count any more'."

109

"But this is a whole battalion, with all the apparatus and official routine of a battalion, established in a semi-permanent camp. We're not cut off from the world in the sense your Company was. We're not all that far from Aden, and we've got a Brigadier coming to visit us on Boxing Day."

"I agree," said Fingel, "that we are somewhat less remote than B Coy was in Korea; so I don't think what you call 'the side-effects' are likely to happen here. But I see no reason why *Fingerella* should not be well received by the men merely as a bawdy romp."

"The moment you start rehearsing, word will go to the Colonel or the Second in Command. And then look out."

"We shall rehearse in secret."

"You'll have to get copies of the script made on the machine in the Orderly Room. As soon as somebody sees the first page – "

" – I'll make my own copies on my own duplicator. That's what Geoffrey Ham did."

"Are you determined to land yourself in trouble?"

"I am determined to obey the orders of the Second in Command. A pantomime he has commanded," said Fingel, "and a pantomime he shall have."

*   *   *   *   *   *

Fingerella, as Fingel had foretold, was well received, indeed rapturously received, by the audience – by all of it, that is, except the Colonel, the Second in Command and our guest, the Brigadier. This latter, a lean and fibrous officer very young for his rank, sulked venomously throughout, but when asked by the Colonel at an early stage if he wanted the show to be stopped, shook his head and ordered that it should carry on. Just before the Finale, however, he rose swiftly to his feet and marched out at 160 to the minute, while the Colonel and the Second in Command (both portly men) tried absurdly to keep step in his wake. Later on, Fingel was sent for.

"I'm off," said Fingel when he reappeared in our quarters; "I've got eight hours to pack and go."

"You do not surprise me. Back to the Depot to tender your resignation? Or to begin five years' hard with the Trucial Oman Scouts?"

"Oh dear me, no, old bean. I'm to catch the RAF Despatch Plane from Aden to Malta. It seems that there is a vacancy at Corps Headquarters there – in Intelligence. Quite a cosy billet, even if the Maltese wines *are* rather coarse, and certainly preferable to this desert. My appointment, by the way, is in the rank of Temporary Lieutenant-Colonel."

"*That's* what the Brigadier had to say to you?"

"Yes. He was asked to nominate someone for the job only the other day. He thinks I'm just the man."

"I don't understand."

"He wants me out of his Brigade, right?'

"Right. But what have you done to deserve promotion and a cushy appointment?"

"More than you might think. You remember my telling you about the Prince in the original production of *Fingerella*?"

"The Senior Lieutenant in your Company? The one who was . . . 'assiduous' in his attentions?"

"That's it. A very assiduous man in everything he did. So assiduous that he is now one of our youngest Brigadiers; *our* Brigadier, in fact. It was interesting to meet him again. He left the battalion soon after Korea and I hadn't seen him since. When I heard he was to take over this Brigade, I said to my-self, 'Perhaps he'll do something for an old chum', but I wasn't quite sure how to . . . jog his powers of recollection. Then, when the Second in Command ordered a pantomime, I suddenly saw my way clear."

"But you tried to refuse to do one."

"Feigned reluctance," said Fingel; "good tactics. The Second in Command was so relieved when he finally got his way with me that he didn't ask any questions about what I intended to cook up . . . which was a *soufflé surprise* for our distinguished guest."

"Sheer blackmail. I'm amazed that he sat so much of it through."

"It lured him down memory lane perhaps, despite himself. And what memories. No wonder he couldn't quite take the Wedding Scene with Fingers in the Finale. It says the last word about the Prince's eccentric tendencies – from which his own were not far removed. Geoffrey Ham was a skilful caster."

"What did the Brigadier *say* when he saw you this afternoon?"

"He was spare of speech. Not a single overt reference to the past. 'This afternoon's production,' he said, 'has convinced me that you would be better employed elsewhere. Your undoubted talents recommend you for promotion.' It was his way of admitting that he *owed* me."

"He has paid very handsomely."

"I suppose so." Fingel sighed and put three handkerchiefs embroidered with my initials into his tin trunk. "I'll be missing you, old bean," he said, "but at my age one can't neglect offers of advancement."

"What are you going to do about your unpaid Mess bills here, and those cheques?"

"The Second in Command, as Mess President, has agreed to write off the bills and tear up the cheques."

"Why on earth?"

"That joke about Dandini and the soldiers' socks. He thinks I put it in as a hint that I've discovered that's *his* little hobby. Now he too is keen to pave my path to external promotion. Which reminds me. Bachelor Colonels," said Fingel, packing my dinner jacket, "will be much in demand on Malta, so I expect I shall be needing this."

Colonel Fingel

Corps HQ,
Malta.
January 4

My dear old bean,

You'll be pleased to hear that Lieutenant-Colonel Fingel has already made rather a hit on Malta. In a discreet way, of course; for its's best behaviour from now on, old bean, at least until they see fit to make my temporary lieutenant-colonelcy substantive. Having this in mind, I decided to give the new-image Fingel a trial trot at the Club Ball on New Year's Eve. Wit without ribaldry, gallantry without salacity, jollity without inebriety – all these were to be the qualities of the sociable off-duty Colonel Fingel, who was also to be a real *pukkha sahib* but without any of the old racialist knobs on. (A mild liberal streak is essential for promotion these days.) So I got myself up a treat in your dinner jacket, introduced myself modestly to my new colleagues, danced with the General's wife and also with his unmarried sister, hinted at a deep, tragic and entirely honourable love affair in my youth which explained why I had remained a bachelor ever since (the girl broke her neck in a hunting accident in the Shires a week before the

wedding and the shock prostrated me for months, etc., etc.),
stood my whack of the harry champers but never so much as
belched the whole evening, and gave an overall impression of
being a twenty-four-carat Buchan character with an interesting
dash of E. Philips Oppenheim. Never has your "soup and fish"
been worn to such elegant advantage.

Things have gone quite well with the "on duty" Colonel
Fingel too. My immediate boss is a mild-mannered Staff
Brigadier whose hobby is butterflies; my job consists in collating
information about the attitudes and behaviour of Arabs along
the Mediterranean coast. I pass my working hours in an old-
fashioned colonial office with a fan and am free to spend nine
out of ten of them reading or doing what I will – *except*
leaving the place for any longer than it takes to have a pee. For
the great bore is that it is very difficult to get time off: the
General is a bit of a martinet and puts the wind up my nice little
Brigadier, who has a neurotic horror of letting me out of my
office (though he knows as well as I do how little I have to do
in it) in case the General should come nosing round and spot
an empty desk. Still, *il faut souffrir un peu pour être colonel*, and
there *are* palpable splendours.

Thus for my quarters, I have two rooms and a private bathroom in HQ A Mess, and a grovelling Maltese servant. The
food is disgusting, but I have found two just tolerable restaurants within half a mile, where I am paying my bills (in accordance with the new career-building Fingel life-style) strictly in
cash. Whose cash, do I hear you enquire? Well, should you
happen to have missed that gold ticker of yours, console yourself with thinking that it fetched £79 for the Feed Fingel Fund
at the top pop shop in Valletta. Sorry, old bean, to be quite so
exploiting, but when you're turning over a new leaf, as I am,
it is necessary to carry substantial assets with you (which is
possibly why so few people ever succeed in turning over a new
leaf).

Tonight, at least, there will be no cash outlay, as I am to
dine with the General – my official welcome to his Staff. I
rather think that sister of his is a bit stuck on me; she certainly

protruded her abdomen pretty forcibly when we danced together at the Ball.

Cheers for now,
Fingel.

Malta,
Jan. 6

Old Bean,

No doubt about it: the General's sister is scorching her panties for Fingel. I think it was that story about my fiancée busting her neck that brought it on; nothing like a spot of melodrama for tuning up bored ladies of a certain age. As it happens, she's not so old but what Fingel could plug himself in with some pleasure; but the new Fingel life-style discourages liaisons with close connections of one's General, and even if it didn't, the General himself certainly would. For I fear he's decoded the message already (there's probably been similar trouble before), and indeed he'd be very slow if he hadn't, because after dinner she sat me down under her enormous photograph album and started playing thighsies beneath it (while showing me pics of her bouncing about on Mombasa beach, etc., a decade or two ago) with all the delicacy of a rhinoceros.

So I got rather a cold good-night from Mr and Mrs General. I hope my efforts at reform are not going to be bitched up by –

– Had to break off just now because my Brigadier sent for me. It seems that I am to be sent on a Mission. The General has picked me to go on a kind of liaison trip in Israel of all places: we're doing a three-month swop of Staff Officers with the Hebrews to promote understanding and good will, tira lira, meaning they'll want to guzzle up all the info I've gathered about the Arabs, so they won't be very pleased when they find out that I've only been in my job for five days. When I put this to the Brigadier, he said that the General was impressed by my personality and trusted me to put up a good show, my lack of knowledge notwithstanding. If you ask me, he's bothered by all the heaving that went on under the album last night and wants to get me out of the way of his sister before she runs her knickers right up to the mast-head. But apparently there's also another reason, one which gave the Brig. some embarrassment.

"The thing is, Fingel," he said, "that they've indicated that they would strongly prefer us to send – well – a Jewish officer, if we have one. They think he would be more sympathetic."

"Well, that counts me out," I said. "I'm about as kosher as a pork pie."

"Oh, you don't have to be absolutely *orthodox*," he said, "they don't expect that. Just Jewish by blood."

"But I'm not," I said. "Ill-bred I may be, but I'm not a bloody Yi – "

" – Please, Fingel," he implored, "don't make it difficult for me. The fact is that we have no Jewish officer available; but your physical appearance is such that you could . . . just . . . pass for Jewish. In an Austrian sort of way. Your name will pass too. We want you to pretend to be Jewish in order to humour them."

"Vat's in it vor me?" I said. "A crown of thorns if they find out the truth?"

"It's no joking matter, Fingel. It's important that we should be on good terms with the Israelis, and you, in a sense, will be our Ambassador."

Of course I could refuse on grounds of conscience, but I've decided to go. After all, if the General wants me off the scene for a while there's no point in staying on it; and anyhow it's one way of getting myself out of this dreary office. There could be credit in the affair if I make myself agreeable to the Chosen; there will certainly be a cash bonus, as I shall be paid a special allowance to put me in funds to cut a suitable figure.

The masquerade begins in three days' time with a flight from here to Tel-Aviv. Meanwhile I'm punching up on my bible. As the Brig. says, although I'm not to wear funny hats or anything weird like that, I must know a bit of my own history, as a Jew, and be prepared to take an interest. Apparently my term of duty will start with a guided tour round the sights of the country, so I must have a few appropriate scriptural gobbets on the tip of my tongue – and also know the difference between the Mishnah and a Mezuzah. And another thing: I've been told off to take an interest, while I'm there, in the sort of things they *won't* be eager to show me, like instances of disaffection or bad morale, or, on the other hand, the state of their advanced rocketry (and tactical atomic weapons, if, as has recently been rumoured, they've found a cheap and easy way of running them up). This means that I have to make my Jewish act go with a real swing, or I'll never get near any apparatus more up to date than a camel.

So this is our man in Jerusalem designate signing off for now. More from the Land of Canaan.

Love from
Fingelstein.

Camp Uriah,
Near Tel-Aviv.
January 10

Dear Bean,

Red carpet time for Fingel. I was given a first-class seat in the aeroplane yesterday afternoon, and waiting at the airport to greet me was a deputation headed by an Israeli Major-General, and further consisting of a gaggle of Staff Colonels and spare Majors and, last but not least, of Second Lieutenant Jael Fezzez (a female), who is to be my driver and general assistant. We all rumbled off in a military charabanc, had dinner in the best non-kosher restaurant in Tel-Aviv, and swept out here to Camp Uriah, where I was installed in a palatial marquee and then briefed about my programme. This, as advertised, is to start with a five-day tour of the Promised Land, conducted by 2/Lt. Fezzez, who will be driving us in a

Land Rover. I didn't take in much about what will happen later, because liberal rations of whisky were being offered; but clearly I'm to be softened up by trips and treats for quite some time to come. Then, I suppose, they'll be on to me for all that Near Eastern Intelligence which I haven't got . . . but that problem can wait.

At this moment, Miss Fezzez is fussing around outside the marquee, counting the kit we're to take and ramming it into the Land Rover. I don't quite know what to make of her, but am rather bothered by the clear disapproval which she showed of the feasting and junketing last night. She's a wide, squat creature, of about twenty years old, very dark and somewhat in need of a shave, with enormous bra-less knockers under her khaki skirt and bandy thighs like nutcrackers, which frequently protrude from under her regulation skirt despite her angry efforts to confine them. Or rather, they did last night, but today she's wearing trousers and combat boots. The boots make her calves look like a pair of caveman's clubs with the bludgeoning ends uppermost, while the trousers strongly assert the bandiness of her hams, which make a broad elipse – nearly a circle – when she is standing to attention. This she insists on doing whenever she talks to me as if to convey the exclusively military nature of our association – which she further proclaims by interspersing her austere and practical remarks with ferocious barks of "sir". Typical conversation:

"You will need one valise, *sir*, which you already have, and two haversacks. The latter, sir, I shall procure for you."

"Surely the valise will be enough, Jael. We're only away for five days."

"I am Second Lieutenant Fezzez, sir, and I am telling you you will need two haversacks to carry water-bottles and hard-tack rations. There are no restaurants, *sir*, in the desert. I shall go now to the store and get the haversacks – and the camp beds."

"Can I help?"

"No, sir. I am quite sufficient to carry two haversacks and two camp beds."

And so she is. I hope the camp beds are for emergency use only.

Nothing overt has yet been said about my being a Yid, but of course I have been billed as such by HQ at Malta and it is absolutely taken for granted that my attitudes will be pro-Jewish and pro-Zionist. Several times last night disparaging references were made to the general characteristics of the "goyim", who did not, I was told, appreciate the Israeli achievement (whereas I, it was implied, was naturally bound to do so). The only "goy" they have much time for is Liddell Hart, whom they seem to regard as the founding father of their Army and the inspiration behind their system of training officers. If 2/Lt Fezzez is representative of the system, Liddell Hart has a lot to answer for: you never saw such a savagely bossing little baggage. She has just announced, "Three minutes and twenty seconds to the start-time, *sir*", so I'd better be on my feet – otherwise she'll lead me to the Land Rover in chains.

> Shalom (which means "peace
> be with you" in these parts,
> not that there is much with
> 2/Lt Fezzez banging about)
> from
> Fingel.

Sodom
Jan. 12

Old Bean,

We're spending tonight in a kind of Government hostel on the shore of the Dead Sea, Sodom being no longer a city but only an encampment for workers on the salt flats. 2/Lt Fezzez wanted to put up a tent and eat hard-tack, and tried to pretend there was nowhere we could stay. But I spotted this hostel place, and told her that *I* was going to dine and sleep in it, and she could bloody well make herself miserable in a tent if she wanted to. Rather to my surprise, she gave in at once and consented to come with me.

But when I think it over, I know perfectly well why she did: she hasn't succumbed to the lure of relative comfort or anything corrupt like that; she's simply determined (in accordance, one supposes, with her orders) not to let me out of her sight. I can hardly go for a widdle without 2/Lt Fezzez tagging on to make sure I don't stumble on Israeli State secrets in the pisser. Why she should want to stick so close to me in Sodom, where there's nothing to see but salt, I can't imagine. But she's staying as near as she can get, in the very next room to my own, on the other side of a very thin partition (probably with a spy hole in it). At this moment she's thumping around singing a nationalistic song in Hebrew and (I hope) putting on something decorative for dinner – I'm heartily sick of those combat boots.

To be fair, though, she's been a very interesting guide. We've been to see lots of good antiquities and visited several important schools and hospitals and so on, and whether what we see is Ancient or Modern she always knows a bit about it and trots it out rather racily. Example (coming into Sodom this evening):

"Sodom was one of the two legendary Cities of the Plain, *sir*, the other being Gomorrah. In Gomorrah" – absolutely po-faced . . . "was pleasure between ladies with instruments, in Sodom was all-male anal intercourse. This made Jehovah so angry that he turned all the perverts into lumps of salt."

I particularly like "ladies with instruments".

What is noticeable, however, is that we have never been near any *military* installations. I keep hinting that I'd like to see some soldierly sights, but all she says is, "That will be for later. This week is for cultural, geographic and civic." And another thing: in between being cultural, geographic and civic, she's trying to pump me. Not about anything important, or even about my coastal Arabs, but about my own attitudes (a) as a Jew to the British Army, (b) as a British officer to the Israeli Army, and (c) as a Jew from outside to Israel. No harm in it, I suppose, but I find it irritating, so I'm trying to pump her back. What was her education? How and why did she become an officer? What's her usual job? Neither of us, I should add, is getting anywhere. Sample, from early this morning:

"How many officers at your Malta Headquarters, sir, are of the Jewish race?"

"Very few, Jael."

"2/Lt Fezzez, please. Is that because the British Army does not like Jews or because Jews do not like the British Army?"

"I don't know. What made *you* choose the Army for a career?"

"In Israel it is different. In Israel, sir, we are all soldiers. How did you find Camp Uriah?"

"I wasn't shown enough of it to say. When are we going to see other Army Camps?"

"I told you. This week, SIR, is for culture. How do you find our roads?"

"Bumpy."

"They are *not* bumpy. They are excellent."

"You'd know better than I. Do you do a lot of this kind of thing?"

"What kind of thing?"

"Driving visiting officers around."

"I have been detailed to drive you, sir, because, as you observe, I speak English."

"Very well too. Where did you learn it?"

"From my teacher. This town we now enter is called Garth. Here there is a factory for socks. . . ."

And so on.

Well, I've no objection to playing quizzing games with Fezzez for the next few days, and I always enjoy this kind of trip, but I'm afraid that I'm not making quite the right impression. Perhaps I'm not enthusiastic enough about the orphanages; perhaps I shouldn't have called the roads bumpy. Whatever the reason, it's clear that Fezzez is not entirely sure of me, is indeed very wary of me, and since she'll be reporting back at the end of our jaunt, it's important that I should change this. If Fezzez gives me the thumbs down, I shall never get near a kosher rocket or even a machine gun; I shall be sent home empty (even perhaps early, if they really take against me) and that will mean the end of any chance of my being made substantive. I've got to mind my 'p's and 'q's, old bean, and above all I've got to stop Fezzez from nosing out that I'm a goy. She's been giving me some pretty close looks, so she may be having her doubts already.

Ah well. Time for our Sodomite din-din. I will say this for Israel – the wines are damned good, if ever Fezzez lets one get near them.

Mene mene tekel upharsin
and love from Fingel

Caesarea
Jan. 14

My dear Bean,

A deadly and ironic twist of fortune. Read and mark.

That night at Sodom, just after I last wrote to you, Fezzez turned out for dinner like Jezebel *en fête*. She'd had the shave she needed; she'd done her hair up in a pile like a pyramid; she'd painted her lips pillar-box red; and she was wearing one of those page-boy tunic things which stop a short way down the thighs – with stockings and suspenders underneath it instead of the usual tights. The last time I'd seen her in a skirt she kept tugging it down: this time she positively rolled out her thighs like barrels. Oh ho, says I to myself, this is the Mata Hari bit; she's dropping the ice curtain and turning temptress in order to get Fingel off his guard.

The worrying thing was that in an awful kind of animal way she was terrifically lust provoking. Those huge expanses of circular sinew – how one ached for their mighty grip, how one longed to feel them shudder like mountains in an earth-quake. That scarlet gash of a mouth – one could almost hear the obscene shrieks of pleasure pouring out of it. But that way, I knew, lay madness and disaster. Colonel Fingel must keep his cool. To go beddy-byes with Second Lieutenants in Sodom would be asking for every kind of trouble in the book.

"Good even, Colonel," she said.

"Good evening, 2/Lt Fezzez."

"Now we know each other better, you should call me Jael."

"Yes – er – Jael."

"I have ordered some wine for us."

"How nice. . . ."

All through dinner she sat with her legs wide apart under the table. I couldn't see this; I just knew, from the way she sat in her chair, that she was straddling like a gorilla. And of course the knowledge was torture. She didn't say much, just grinned with her red mouth and poured about a gallon of wine into it. Then, over the coffee, she came right to the point.

"Colonel Fingel, I am randy for you."

"Randy" really finished me off. If I didn't have her I was going to go off bang. Never mind being substantive, never mind anything. Anynow, I told myself, perhaps I'd been thinking too cautiously: for after all, if I made a good job of it, she'd be on my side from now on, she'd give me a good chitty when asked to report to the brass-hats, and I might yet get to see a rocket-launcher or even an Atomic Shell.

"Me too," I said.

"Come then."

But as I followed her fesses out of the dining-room, a dreadful thought struck me. Let us put it like this: you can have a circumcised goy but you can't have an uncircumcised Jew. At some stage in our imminent intimacy, Jael was bound to find out that Fingel was a Philistine. Indeed, that might well be what the whole act was in aid of: suspecting that I was not really Jewish, 2/Lt Fezzez, glutton for duty as she was, had settled on a simple means of securing proof. But it was too late to retreat now, for if I did she would certainly guess why, and then the fat would be in the fire without even the fun of frying it first.

Then it occurred to me that I might get away with it if I pretended to extreme diffidence, insisted on absolute darkness, and somehow dissuaded her from preliminary manipulation. Or again, I thought, at moments of really high tension the distinction between Cavalier and Roundhead is less easily made by investigating parties. But despite such minor consolations I was anything but confident, as I slunk after her into her room, of my capacity to pass myself off on her as the genuine Semitic article.

I need not have worried. As I entered, she slammed the door behind me, ripped off her tunic with a snort, and advanced on me like an ogre at feeding time.

"And now, my lovely Colonel Goy," she said, "I am going to undress you with these hands."

She'd guessed, you see. She'd been brooding on the matter for some time, and earlier that day, when I'd shown myself indifferent to the question of why there are so few Jews in the British Army, she'd rumbled me flat. Any real Jew, questioned by another Jew about such a topic, would have carried on about it for a day and a half. I'd just dismissed the thing, *ergo* I could not be Jewish – and that, as it turned out, was what had turned her on. She was sick of neatly cut cocks, old bean; she wanted a goy's toy to play with for a change. Heaven knows what had happened to her patriotism and her sense of duty. She just seemed to toss them off as briskly as she tossed off her knickers.

"Thanks be to Jahveh in Jerusalem," she mouthed as she yanked down my trousers, "at last a proper roll of schmotter."

And then she was off.

And now here we are, two days later, in Caesarea. Old bean, I was almost too exhausted, when we arrived, even to look at the famous statue of the Emperor Augustus (the only one which unambiguously shows his deformity). Old bean, *Jael will not stop*. Even when she's driving, she'll stick a muscular hand across for a quick bout of heavy – and I mean heavy – petting. It's like living with a vampire – only it's not my blood she's draining. Old bean, I am at my wits' end. Whenever I try to refuse to play, or to insist on something in return – like just the teeniest piece of intelligence about Israeli armaments – she simply threatens, if I do not comply most minutely with her filthiest urges, to show me up to her superiors as not being a Jew. The choice, then, is between being discredited and dismissed from Israel (without a jot of information to show for it) or being ground to death by this Hebrew Messalina. Whatever

"*And now, my lovely Colonel Goy, I am going to undress you with these hands.*"

shall I do? Quite apart from anything else, she is also beginning
to need another shave.

Yours *de profundis*
Fingel

Kibbutz Aleph,
Near Lake Tiberias
Jan. 15

My Bean,

My last was written yesterday afternoon, from the very pit
of despair, as you will probably have noticed. Since then two
things have happened, one good and one bad.

The good thing is that 2/Lt Fezzez has now succumbed to the
circling of the moon and will not be molesting me for a while.
Apparently she suffers more than most from lunar trouble;
certainly she was very low as she drove me up here from
Caesarea. It will take a good two days to restore her enthusiasm,
by which time we should be back at Camp Uriah, where she
will no longer have me to herself and evasion will be easier in
consequence.

You will observe, however, that I write "should" be back in
Camp Uriah (where we are due tomorrow) and you will
correctly deduce a shade of doubt. This brings us to the bad
thing that has happened. We arrived, early this evening, at
Kibbutz Aleph, which is a sort of propaganda show-place
situated not far from the banks of the Jordan and just south of
the Sea of Galilee. Very pretty, very fertile, full of libraries,
school-rooms and ping-pong tables, this kibbutz is used as an
enticement to European Jews who are thinking of going Zionist
and might not be quite so keen if they were shown one of the
really rugged set-ups in the desert. But there is one trouble with
Aleph: it's altogether too near the firing line, and indeed was
very nastily raided by Arabs some years ago. For this reason
they keep a twenty-four-hour piquet going; but at the same
time, since they want visitors to get a peaceful impression, they
don't parade a guard in uniform, they just send the shifts

sidling off to the outworks in civilian clothes, as if they were going off to pick oranges or something. When the shifts reach the trenches or whatever they take over the arms of the previous shift, and so no guest at Aleph is ever subjected to the sight of weaponry or otherwise alarmed in any way.

Unless, that is, the alarm is actually sounded – which it was this evening, ten minutes after Jael had booked us into our chalets. As I was sinking down into a much needed nap, being still heavily *souffrant* from the labours of Jael even though these had been suspended for the last twenty-four hours by the onset of her lunar affliction – as I was sinking down, I say, into blissful, hoggish slumber, a siren blew off like a hooter from hell, and one of the piquet, who was just going on duty, came running into my chalet to tell me to accompany him to the trenches, where he doubtless thought Colonel Fingel would be an asset. But since, as I've told you, the piquet are without uniform and without weapons until they have actually taken over their positions from their predecessors, I had no idea who this johnny was and told him pretty sharply to take himself off and to knock politely next time he wanted to enter a gentleman's chalet – adding a few Fingelian refinements for good measure. (Silly of me; I should have known from that damned hooter more or less what was up.) Well, as it happened the alarm was false and the very next second a countermanding blast was blown for all clear; but by that time the damage was done. As Israelis count these matters, I had been overbearing and un-comradely in attitude; I had assumed privilege of rank; I had been unalert, idle, irresponsible and possibly cowardly in the face of enemy attack; and I had accused a fellow Jew of "banging in here like a whole herd of Gadarene swine" – which is about as tactful as spitting in Church. It only goes to show what happens if you drop your guard for one second – as I should never have done, of course, had I not been so debilitated by the monstrous antics of Jael Fezzez.

But then I've only got myself to thank for letting *that* start in the first place. No good trying to shift the blame. Anyway, the fact of the matter, *now*, is that sour and priggish countenances are being trained on the leper Fingel from every corner of this damned kibbutz. Dinner in the communal dining-room was a nightmare. Jael says that the head of the place has already rung up Camp Uriah to complain about my conduct, and she scathingly opines that I'll be shipped back to Malta in disgrace and direct from Aleph. A decision will be promulgated by telephone from Camp Uriah tomorrow morning. At least, if they pack me back to Malta, I shall escape from Jael's blackmailing groin-hold and a lingering death by sexual erosion. But it also means the end of my hopes of a substantive lieutenant-colonelcy – and probably the end of the temporary rank as well. Oi voi . . . perhaps I was never cut out for a colonel. I'll write later to tell you the exact manner of my going. I only hope they make it quick.

Yours from the wailing wall
Fingel

Camp Uriah
Jan. 17

Old Bean,

Saved by the bell (if only to fight another round).

Very late on the night of Fingel's disgrace at Aleph, Jael had second thoughts. She realised that her indisposition would soon be over and that then she'd be razor-keen for Fingel again. However much she may despise me for my behaviour during the dud alarm, my goyish charms are still too novel to be dispensed with. This or something very near it is the only conceivable explanation of what followed.

On the morning after the hurly-burly, the expected telephone call came through from Camp Uriah. 2/Lt Fezzez was to take me to Tel-Aviv and park me in the worst hotel; she was then to collect the remnant of my kit from the Camp, along with an economy-class air ticket to Malta, and see me on to the first plane out. Very much what Jael had foretold but not at all what she now wanted. So she invented a tale to save Fingel's blushing face. What happened was all her fault, she said to the head of the kibbutz, because she had upset me: she had laughed in my face, on the way down from Lake Galilee, because I had made a declaration of passionate love and asked her to marry me. Her mockery had so distressed me that at last she had taken pity – to the extent of administering an outsize tranquilliser when we arrived at the kibbutz. What with the tranquilliser, therefore, and what with my emotional crisis still bubbling away underneath its incipient effect, I had been in no condition, when the alarm went, to know where I was or what I was doing. Hence my tantrum when obtruded upon by the piquet. She (Jael) had not mentioned all this the night before because she had been rather ashamed of her behaviour (and of course I had been much too much of a gentleman to raise the matter on my part); but now she realised it was her duty to speak out for me. Would the head of the kibbutz (Jael concluded) now be so good as to ring up Camp Uriah, explain what had really happened and get permission for her to return there that day with Colonel Fingel in accordance with the original schedule?

Quite a cunning wheeze. The story was flattering to the charm of Israeli girlhood (a subject on which they need constant reassurance, as so many of their girls are just like Jael), and it also set me up in a pleasing light – as the Jew (supposed) who had behaved with the chivalry of an English gentleman and was prepared to suffer obloquy rather than impugn a lady's name. The ruse worked. The head of the kibbutz telephoned the military, Fingel was deemed to be rehabilitated, and off we set in the Land Rover, Jael and I, heading south for Camp Uriah.

But now I was back with my original problem. I had not been saved so much as merely preserved, like a fruit, for Jael's future consumption. As she drove, she babbled happily about the three months of ecstasy which lay before us. Already the effects of the moon were wearing off, as her demeanour made alarmingly plain, and almost any time now she might be ready for more action. It was now or never: if I did not find means of controlling her or disposing of her, by the next day at the very latest those nutcracker thighs would have my poor old carcase in thrall once more. What made it worse was that her hold on me was now doubled: not only could she blow up my pretence of being Jewish, she could at any time unsay what she'd said to save my face at Kibbutz Aleph. *Or could she?* After all, she'd dived in pretty deep –

– And then I suddenly saw how I could turn the tables. When we reached Camp Uriah, I would seek an interview with the Commandant. . . .

". . . Sir," I said to him, "you have heard what led to the unfortunate incident at Kibbutz Aleph?"

"We have heard that you were not yourself, and why."

"Exactly. I had proposed marriage to 2/Lt Fezzez and been turned down. In the circumstances, you will understand that a continued association must be embarrassing to both of us. Could you possibly find another junior officer to act as my aide from now on?"

The Commandant saw my point. 2/Lt Fezzez, praise be to Jahveh in Jerusalem, has been tactfully posted elsewhere, and has disappeared without a murmur; for in fact, old bean, she never had any hold on me at all: she could hardly show me up as a goy without explaining how she came by her proof, and she could hardly denounce my behaviour at Aleph without revealing that her previous defence of me was a ramping fib, told, as would rapidly have been discovered, from erotic partiality to Fingel. Her threat had always been futile; thank God I tumbled to this in time – if only just.

Fezzez' replacement has now arrived, a lieutenant on the reserve doing her annual spell of service. This will be her last tour of duty, despite the exigent needs of her country, as she is nearly fifty-seven years old, rapidly balding, and (she tells me proudly) five times a grandmother. Tomorrow Granny and I set off on a gentle trip to Joppa, where I am to be taken over an orange-crating depot. I don't seem to be getting much nearer to spotting rockets, but at least I'm still in one piece and more or less *bien vu*, which is saying a lot after the events of the past week.

Shalom, old bean, it's peace at last
for Fingel

O Bean, Bean,

Now I've seen everything.

After finishing and posting my last, and sucking down six soothing whiskies, I turned in for the night in my marquee. Hardly had my head hit the pillow, when there was a scratching at the entrance flap and then a voice in my ear, which said,

"Move over, little Colonel, and make room for your new comrade" —

GRANNY.

Whether *she'd* guessed I was a goy, I don't know, but in any case she was delighted with what she found, and the old girl certainly knew a trick or two, I'll say that for her. So I was just resigning myself to my new fate, when there was another scratch at the flap and a voice said,

"I am not to leave after all until dawn tomorrow. We have five last wonderful hours" —

FEZZEZ.

Whereupon Granny croaked that she'd arrived too late, and Fezzez yanked naked Granny out of the sack with one flick of her wrist, and Granny toppled Jael with a smart left hook, ripping her shirt from her back as she went, and before you could say Nebuchadnezzar these two butch Jewesses were milling away like tarts in a cowboys' brothel, screaming insults to match. Thirty seconds later the piquet arrived. Fezzez and Granny were swept off still screeching like a pair of drunken parrots, and a little later I was summoned without ceremony to explain the affair to the Field Officer of the Week, who had been roused by the piquet commander. Explanation there was none fit to offer. I had my quietus next morning from the Commandant, who put the whole thing in a nutshell:

"One way or another, Colonel Fingel, you seem to have an unsettling effect on my officers, however carefully selected. I fear you must return to Malta."

From Malta I am to be returned, as "superfluous to any

credible requirement" (the General's phrase), to the Regimental Depot. What the future holds I don't yet know, but it certainly holds no colonelcies, substantive or other,

for Major Fingel.

Now that I am for ever beyond Jael's reach, I begin to miss her. For sheer ball-basteing mischief those daughters of Abraham beat everybody bar the monkeys.

F.

Fingel's Aunt

"That woman must be put down," Fingel said.

"That woman" was Mrs H. I. J. Peregrine-Pierce, wife of Lieutenant-Colonel H. I. J. Peregrine-Pierce OBE, our new Commanding Officer. He had joined our battalion, and so, most emphatically, had she, on our return from the East in the summer of 1967. Almost his first act as CO had been to call an officers' conference in the Mess to discuss the conduct of the functions and entertainments with which we were to celebrate our reappearance in England. To everyone's surprise, Mrs Peregrine-P. had turned up at the conference with him, indeed (as Fingel was later to remark) had virtually marched him into it; and then, having listened with fingers drumming while her husband read out a list of the proposed arrangements, had proceeded to harangue the meeting herself.

"As Senior Wife," she said (we could hear the capital letters), "I am responsible for the Tone of the Regiment's Social Occasions. To a considerable extent this depends on the bearing of the Younger and Unmarried officers, whom I shall now instruct in their Duties during the forthcoming celebrations." She produced a list. "Major Fingel and Major Raven," she barked, "follow me. Others will be called when wanted."

And so Fingel and I had followed her into the Mess Secretary's office, where she seated herself behind the desk and inspected us much as the proprietress of a French provincial restaurant inspects a customer who proffers a cheque.

"You are both nearly forty years old," she said suddenly, "and both still single. Why is that?"

Fingel's eyes began to glint.

"'A soldier'," he suggested lazily, "'is better accommodated than with a wife.' Shakespeare."

"Then I do not agree with Shakespeare," she said, looking like a rat-trap, "and neither, you will find, does Colonel Peregrine-Pierce. Once an officer is over twenty-five, he should put away childish things and settle down with a suitable partner. Officers who remain unmarried give examples of selfishness and extravagance. And often much worse," she said, and snapped her mouth shut like a shrike crushing a beetle.

"Well, I'm sorry," said Fingel, "but I'm afraid I haven't got round to it yet. The men in our family usually favour marriage at about fifty . . . when they've been about long enough to pick something cosy and harmless."

"I have been apprised," hissed the Colonel's lady, "that your last commanding officer was indulgent towards bachelors and their attitudes. This will no longer be the case."

"So I gather, ma'am," said Fingel. "But I don't quite see what all this has to do with our forthcoming celebrations."

"If too many bachelors of mature age are present, they will create a bad impression of the Regiment; they will give it a disreputable air."

"Then perhaps we'd better go on leave."

"You have just been on your disembarkation leave." She knew it all, of course. "In any case, you and those like you" – a contemptuous glance at me – "will be needed to make up the numbers."

"To the disrepute, you say, of the Regiment?"

"Not," she said, in a sharp, steady clack, "if you behave as you should. If you pay the right kind of attentions to the right kind of girls – *eligible* girls, Major Fingel – and if you give it to be plainly understood that now you are back in England you are hoping to settle down, as we expect of you, in the normal manner, then all will be well. The same" – she nearly spat – "applies to you, Major Raven. Now return to my husband's conference, and tell Captain Rowley and Captain Bootle to come in here to me."

In such manner had we been admonished and dismissed; and now, later the same day . . .

"That woman must be put down," said Fingel, "we must shove our swedes together, old bean, and make a plan. . . ."

Phase I of Fingel's plan was Fingel's bachelor dinner. This took place, at a delectable restaurant ten miles away, immediately after Colonel and Mrs Peregrine-P.'s inaugural cocktail party, and thus ensured that most of the "eligible girls" were deserted at 7.30 sharp as all the young officers trooped off to the banquet promised by Fingel. Although the Colonel's lady was observed to be looking more than ever like a rat-trap the next morning, she kept silence for that time.

Phase II was implemented at the cricket match v. the Gentlemen of the county. Fingel and I and a number of the bachelors were playing in this (more or less on our merits), and as long as we were in the field we were safe; but while the Regiment was batting those of us who were out or waiting to go in were supposed to perform such duties as carrying lemonade to and fro for the "eligible girls" and directing their mothers "to the Mess" (i.e. to the lavatory). Fingel's plan, however, consisted in summoning all the bachelors to practise in the nets (on the plausible ground that we must "put up a good show against the county") and co-opting any of those that were dismissed from the middle to bowl at those who had yet to bat. Except for the mere thirty minutes of the tea interval, therefore, the eligible girls were largely unattended. Once again, the Colonel's lady kept her own counsel; but there was a fleck in her eye which made me think that a counter-coup was surely impending.

At Phase III Fingel played his master-stroke. He invited to the ball (the climacteric function of them all) a certain Mrs Offenden, whom he had first met and appreciated while we were in Kenya and she was touring Africa. "Auntie" Offenden, as Fingel called her behind her back (especially when he was boasting of the lavish presents which he scrounged off her on plea of penury), was a lady of ample if somewhat over-ripe physical attractions, who acknowledged no tiresome obligations to Mr Offenden (something in the City) and was yet respectable enough, being the occasional guest of minor royalty, to be invited anywhere. She was jolly, worldly and witty; she was easygoing and undemanding, with a smile discreetly lewd; she was a feather in any bachelor's cap – the very image of what a soldier was better accommodated with than a wife.

Fingel had widely and assiduously advertised the forthcoming appearance of "my Auntie Offenden", and had engaged her for two purposes (apart, that is, from his carnal and pecuniary ones) : to demonstrate publicly his unassailable preference for his present way of life, and in order to distract his brother officers from the eligible girls provided by Mrs Peregrine-Pierce. For a time all went Fingel's way at the ball: the unmarried captains clustered round Mrs Offenden, and even the shyest subaltern (encouraged by her thigh-caressing smile) led her out to waltz. As for the Colonel's lady, she was receiving Fingel's message loud and clear; but, as heretofore during their contest, she was biding her time. She bided it, in fact, until just after supper . . . when she was observed tapping Colonel P-P. on the shoulder, whispering intently in his ear, and then giving him a smart shove in the direction of the Offenden/Fingel group. The group parted; the Colonel requested a dance; Mrs O. rose like Semiramis to comply.

"It is a special pleasure," the Colonel said, "to welcome a close relation of Major Fingel's."

"A close what of Major Fingel's?" said Mrs Offenden, stopping short of the floor.

"Relation. His aunt, surely."

"His *aunt*?"

"They tell me he is always talking of his rich and generous aunt. 'Dear old Auntie Offenden,' he is always saying, 'she's just sent me another £50 – should be enough for a dinner . . .'."

But already Fingel's Auntie Offenden had turned from the Colonel and dealt Fingel such an epic back-hander as made the teeth rattle in his chops and the champagne glass shatter in his fist; after which she marched out of the ball and out of her nephew's bank account for ever.

The Passing of Fingel

The day Fingel retired from the Army he gave a party at our Regimental Depot in Salop.

"Twenty-five years with the Colours, give or take a few days," he said the day before; "one may as well do the right thing for once. Drinks for all chums *ad lib.* and after dinner; always the best time. I've got permission from the Commandant to invite Mack into the Mess and one or two of the Warrant Officers."

In fact Fingel could perfectly well have stayed on in the Service for another ten years, until he was fifty-five. Even though he was now stuck fast in the rank of Major, the Army could have continued to find work, of a kind, to fill in his time – was indeed bound to do so if he wished to remain.

"But what work?" he had said to me some time before. "Counting spare parts or auditing Mess accounts. Not my world, old bean. Time to go."

"But whatever are you going to do?" I had asked him.

"Commute my pension – that'll raise a few thou – and stick the lot on some horse. If I'm lucky I'll then have a comfortable capital, and if it goes wrong I can slit my throat."

"Jokes apart, Fingel: *what* are you going to *do?*"

"I've just told you."

"Please be serious. Now, what about your mother's money?"

"I'm beginning to think she's immortal. In any case, it's just not enough, old bean, to keep Fingel in the manner to which he wishes to become accustomed. Or not for more than a few months."

"But with your share of that, when it comes, *and* your pension, *and* your gratuity – "

" – I could just about find enough fuel to crawl down the years to my grave – "

" – *And* what you could earn in the sort of job open to ex-officers – "

" – Like secretary to a suburban golf club, grovelling to a pack of haberdashers? You look here, old bean: I'm leaving the Service because I've now reached the stage at which it can offer me only boring and humiliating tasks; so it surely stands to reason I don't aim to be bored and humiliated outside it. Give me liberty, as the man said, or give me death."

And so now, on the day of Fingel's farewell party, I still had no idea of his plans. All I knew was that he would be paid a gratuity of three or four thousand pounds down, and that he would receive a modest annual pension, half of which (and only half) he would be able to commute "for a few thou" more. In whatever way he arranged all that, he would have to have occupation; and on the subject of occupation he simply declined to speak.

"Where are you going tomorrow?" I said, as he held a final inspection of the rows of bottles.

"Somewhere well clear of my mother," was all the indication he would give. "Here's Sweenie Mack. I thought he'd be the first to show up."

It was a good party as such parties go. Most of the guests got drunk, and all the Sergeant-Majors told Fingel, as is their wont on these occasions, that he was the finest officer they'd ever served under. The Commandant handsomely conceded, though not without undertones of irony, that the Regiment would not be the same without him; and several old enemies arrived uninvited and insisted on shaking hands with Fingel and drinking his liquor to his future. Everything, in short, was going off in a more or less decent and traditional fashion, when Sergeant Mack came up to me (at about half past midnight) wearing a worried look.

"There's something wrong about His Honour tonight," Mack said; "I can always tell."

"I expect he's a bit sad."

"No; it's not that, surr; he's fey."

"Pissed?"

"Fey. Meaning, surr, that he's up to some folly, or soon will be. Has His Honour said aught to you, surr, about putting all his pension on a horse?"

"Yes, but he couldn't mean it seriously. Anyhow, he can only commute half his pension, and he can't have done so yet. It takes months to arrange."

"He could have raised money against his pension from somewhere, surr. And against his gratuity too. If not from the bank, from the Hebrews. It wouldna be the first time he's been there. His wurd to me was that he had an eye to some horse at Liverpool."

"He must have meant the Grand National. That's not for weeks yet."

"Exactly so, surr. The earlier you bet, the longer the odds on the ante-post market. It's long odds His Honour seeks."

"Where is he anyway?"

"He was passing round the whusky not three minutes gone. Foreby His Honour is in the lavvy."

But the time passed and His Honour did not return. I sought him in "the lavvy" and then in his bedroom. In the former a sole subaltern was being sick; in the latter Fingel's black tin trunk was sitting on the floor, packed but still open. Automatically I looked into it and retrieved three of my evening shirts. Then I sat on Fingel's bed, gazing stupidly at the trunk, remembering the journeys on which it had accompanied us and the grotesque or scandalous objects which Fingel had from time to time produced from it: native beer, tinned curries, endless stolen goods, a bundle of dildoes which he had picked up for a song in Singapore and hoped to sell (after demonstration) to frustrated Regimental wives whose husbands were away on courses.

As I gazed and remembered, something caught my eye. The removal of my shirts had revealed the jacket of Fingel's Mess Dress. On the left breast of this was pinned a short row of miniature medals: the Coronation Medal (for Fingel had carried the Regimental Colour in the procession, I now recalled), campaign medals for Korea and Kenya. But surely, I thought to myself, those miniatures should be in their case. The case itself, some six inches by two inches and oval in section, was protruding from a sock in which it had been wrapped. Without thinking, I crossed to the trunk, picked out the case and opened it. Inside were about ten pills, little tubular capsules with powder inside them.

"Careful, old bean," said Fingel's voice: "I wouldn't want to lose any of those. A portable cure for all ills."

"Where have you been? I was looking for you."

"Taking a last look round the old place."

He took the medal case from me and put it in his pocket.

"Time to go back to the party," he said.

"Sweenie Mack's worried. He thinks you're up to something."

"Let's go and cheer him up."

We descended the stairs to the room in which the party had been going on. Now only Sergeant Mack remained. Fingel poured himself whisky – his measure for special occasions.

"A final toast," he said: "to the horse I've backed at Liverpool to win my fortune."

"Fingel . . . how much have you put on it?"

"All I could raise on my legitimate expectations."

Mack looked at me as if to say "I told you so".

"What's it called, Your Honour?"

"Just . . . horse." He produced the medal case from his pocket and took out a capsule. "Would you care for a sample? Very stimulating, I'm told, but apt to become addictive, so I don't use it myself. Anyway, I don't believe in consuming my

142

potential profits." He grinned widely. "Horse . . you must have heard the term?"

"Fingel . . . how much of that stuff have you got?"

"Rather a lot. In the bottom of my trunk. I'm keeping these pills separate to interest my customers."

"But where in God's name did you get it?"

"I told you. Liverpool. I met a man in Hong Kong when we were there. He gave me an address and a letter of introduction — told me they were always glad of reliable recruits. I'm working on commission, but if you've got some money to invest they'll let you buy a certain amount at relatively low rates to sell on your own account. They believe in keeping their employees happy, you see. Worker participation, I think it's called."

"No wonder you were cagey about your future. Why are you telling us now?"

"Because I'll be off in ten minutes and you're not going to see me again. In my new game, old bean, one needs to be anonymous and elusive. So Fingel is about to vanish. In a year or two Fingel — or rather, whatever he is then called — should be rich enough to retire. But not in England, I fancy; they're so unkind here to people with unexplained money. Bung-ho." He drunk down his whisky. "My car's outside the Mess," he said: "I brought it over from the garages just now. Do me one last good turn, both of you: help me down with my trunk."

A few minutes later Fingel and his black tin trunk drove away into the darkness. I have neither seen nor heard of him since.